To DIE For

ANNE SCHRAFF

SADDLEBACK
PUBLISHING

URBAN UNDERGROUND

Bad Blood
Dark Secrets
Dark Suspicions
Deliverance
Guilt Trip
Hurting Time
I'll Be There
Leap of Faith
The Lost
Misjudged

No Fear
The Stranger
Time of Courage
To Catch a Dream
To Die For
Unbroken
The Unforgiven
Vengeance
The Water's Edge
Winners and Losers

SADDLEBACK
P U B L I S H I N G
www.sdlback.com

ISBN-13: 978-1-62250-765-8
ISBN-10: 1-62250-765-7
eBook: 978-1-61247-976-7

Printed in Guangzhou, China
NOR/1213/CA21302313

18 17 16 15 14   1 2 3 4 5

CHAPTER ONE

Ernesto Sandoval was finishing his oatmeal before heading for Cesar Chavez High School. He had to turn in a big project for his AP History class. Mr. Quino Bustos, the teacher, was very demanding, and Ernesto was nervous. He had a senior class meeting at the end of the week too, and since Ernesto was senior class president, he was thinking about that a lot.

Suddenly, Ernesto's mother, Maria Sandoval, let out a small cry of dismay. "Oh my," she said, "how sad."

The local television news was on, and Ernesto had been paying no attention to it until now. "What happened, Mom?" he asked, turning toward the screen.

1

"That poor homeless man who hangs out behind Hussam's store ... he was found dead this morning," Maria Sandoval said.

Luis Sandoval, Ernesto's father who taught history at Chavez High, looked up from his eggs. "Poor guy. Probably had a heart attack or maybe he overdosed. I saw him just a few days ago. He was breathing really hard. He asked for change, and thank God I gave him a couple bucks. I'd feel bad if I'd turned him down, and he was so close to the end."

Ernesto's sisters, nine-year-old Katalina and seven-year-old Juanita, were looking at the television screen intently now.

"The news said the police were looking into it," Juanita said. "What's a 'homicide'?"

A worried looked passed through Mrs. Sandoval's eyes. "They think he might not have died of natural causes ... that, you know, somebody killed him," she said.

"That's awful," Katalina said. "He never hurt anybody. Why would somebody kill him?"

Ernesto had spoken to the homeless man—Griff Slocum—a few times. Like his father, Ernesto had given him a few dollars. Griff was very hard to understand. He had a severe speech defect, and he talked softly, barely above a whisper. His head was shaved, and he had a scar on his chin. He looked gaunt, especially in the oversized clothing he usually wore. Ernesto and his best friend, Abel Ruiz, had bought Griff a sub sandwich and coffee a few times, and the man always smiled gratefully and bowed.

"The guy was completely nonviolent," Ernesto said. "One day, I was passing him when somebody gave him a shove and said street people should all be put in jail. He shoved Griff so hard that he almost lost his balance and fell in the street. Griff didn't fight back. He just cowered."

"When was this, Ernie?" his father asked.

"Oh, last year. I gave the mean dude a dirty look and pretended I was taking his

3

picture on my cell phone, and he ran. I never saw him again," Ernesto said.

Ernesto had planned to take his girlfriend, Naomi Martinez, to the mall this afternoon, so he wasn't jogging to school as usual. He drove his Volvo over to the Martinez house to pick up Naomi so they could ride to school together. When Ernesto rapped on the door, he heard Naomi shout, "Come on in, Ernie. I'm almost ready."

When Ernesto went in, he saw Linda Martinez, Naomi's mother, coming from the kitchen. "Hi, Ernie. I'm making cookies for a bake sale," she said.

"Did you hear about Griff Slocum?" Ernesto asked in a voice loud enough for Naomi to hear in her bedroom.

"What about Griff Slocum?" Naomi shouted from the other room.

Naomi came down the hall, looking beautiful as usual. Ernesto caught his breath. "He was found dead in an alley," Ernesto said. "The homicide guys are investigating."

"They think he was murdered?" Linda Martinez asked in a shocked voice.

"I don't know, but there must be some reason why the homicide guys were brought in," Ernesto said.

As they drove the short distance to Cesar Chavez High School, Ernesto recalled how Rod Garcia and Clay Aguirre, two of his least favorite seniors, had been so sure Griff Slocum was guilty in that break-in and shooting at the Torres house. Ernesto and Clay had bad blood between them because Clay had once dated Naomi Martinez and Ernesto took her from Clay—but only after Clay had abused her. And Ernesto had beat Rod Garcia out of senior class president, a job Rod thought he deserved.

"I bet Clay and Rod won't shed any tears over poor Griff," Ernesto said. "They're both down on the homeless people, especially Rod. When he sees one, he acts like the guy is some feral animal or something. I'd seen him taunting Griff and another guy."

5

"Yeah," Naomi said. "A lot of people resent the homeless. Some of them *are* pretty aggressive asking for money, but Griff never was. He'd ask in that small, mumbling voice, as if he were ashamed to be asking at all. The poor guy seemed like somebody life had really dumped on. I felt sorry for him. Who wants to sleep in alleys and look for stuff in dumpsters?"

"Yeah," Ernesto said. "With all the work we do in school, you'd think if you got educated, did it all by the books, life would fall into place, and you'd never have a problem. Sure, that's the ideal thing to do, but sometimes life throws you a curve. What if you got a mental illness? What if the company you worked at for ten years downsizes or sends your job overseas? So much can happen. I don't know what Griff's story was, but nobody chooses to be like that."

"Yeah," Naomi said, "like those kids in our mentoring program. They're only fourteen years old, and they're dealing with so much already."

When he became senior class president, Ernesto started a senior-to-senior tutoring program to help seniors in academic trouble. He also launched a program where seniors mentored at-risk freshmen. Ernesto mentored a student named Richie Loranzo, who was orphaned when his father killed his mother. Richie now lived in foster care. Naomi mentored Angel Roma, daughter of a single mother and granddaughter of a lady very sick with Parkinson's disease. Abel Ruiz mentored Bobby Padilla, who'd run away from a troubled family.

Ernesto wondered what Griff Slocum had been like when he was fourteen. Maybe he had dealt with problems, and nobody had ever reached out to him. Or maybe his problems had been so deep and terrible that he was almost beyond help.

Ernesto parked in the student parking lot at Chavez, and he and Naomi started walking toward the school.

Clay Aguirre had just pulled up in his brand new Hyundai Equus that his parents had just got for him. It was the most expensive car on campus. Ernesto couldn't imagine why anybody would want to drive a car like that at a school where kids were so poor; if they had a car at all, it was a beater. Why did Clay want to be in everybody's face like that?

"So that bum finally bit the dust, huh?" Clay Aguirre said when he neared Ernesto. Clay was handsome, and he made decent grades. He was also a good football player. He was going out with a beautiful senior, Mira Nuñez. Both Ernesto and Naomi thought the girl was crazy for hanging with Aguirre.

"If you mean Griff Slocum is dead, that's not something to celebrate, man," Ernesto said.

"Why not?" Clay snapped. "What good was he? A dirty old bum looking for handouts all the time. A dirty drifter is all he was. What was he contributing to society? He had no right to keep on breathing, dude. He finally did something good. He croaked."

"Clay," Naomi said, "we have no right to judge people like that. A couple weeks ago, my dad saw Griff shivering in the cold, and he stopped and gave the guy an old, worn-out but warm jacket he didn't want anymore. He and Griff were about the same size, and it was a nice warm jacket, better than anything Griff had. He was so grateful he almost kissed my father's hand." Naomi had tears in her eyes.

"We saw him wearing the jacket almost every day. Griff gave my father the opportunity to do something kind, and for that reason alone, Griff's life was worthwhile. He was the reason a lot of people extended a kindness to him, things they wouldn't have done otherwise. Dad was going to throw that jacket in the trash."

"That's a crock," Clay said. "If you want to do something good, give money so smart kids can go to college and be an asset. Don't even waste a ratty old coat on a bum."

Ernesto turned and glared at Clay, "Listen up, man. We got a great program here at Chavez where seniors help each other out. You're good in math. How come you haven't signed up? And what about helping an at-risk freshman? I notice you're not in that either, so what good things do you do, Clay? Ride around in a fancy car flipping off kids in beaters? Is that your good deed?" he said.

Clay Aguirre's eyes narrowed. "I haven't got time for your stupid little do-gooder projects. If some dope can't figure out algebra by himself, he's going nowhere anyway. And the at-risk fresh-men are losers too. That's the trouble with you, Sandoval. You like to hang with losers 'cause, deep down, you're a loser too. You got all these big ideas of being a lawyer, but you got a loser mentality, man. You ain't going nowhere," Clay said. "I play great football, and that's what Chavez High is all about."

"Oh, great, as long as we can rah-rah for the home team, who cares what other prob-lems we're ignoring," Ernesto said bitterly.

"You know why you hate football, dude?" Clay said with a sneer. "Because you're too much of a wimp to play a rough game like that. You're a coward, Sandoval. That's why you put on those little short pants and run on the track team. You haven't got the balls put your body on the line against guys who outweigh and outmuscle you, coming at you like wild bulls. That's my meat and potatoes."

"I don't hate football," Ernesto said calmly, in spite of the anger boiling inside him. "I just don't like some of the guys who play it."

"Come on, Ernie," Naomi said with disgust on her face. "This is a big waste of time. We'll be late for class."

By the end of the day, they still had not learned the cause of Griff Slocum's death, but he had suffered a serious blow to his head. Witnesses who found the body said he was bleeding profusely from a gash in his head. They said the injury was much

11

too severe to have been caused by a fall. An autopsy was scheduled. In the meantime, the police were asking any possible witnesses to Griff Slocum's final hours to come forward. He had died between midnight and four in the morning on Washington Street near Tremayne.

When Ernesto got home that day, he heard quite a bit about Griff Slocum on the local news. Nobody in the *barrio* knew much about the man, but just about everybody knew who he was. He had become a fixture on Washington Street by Hussam's store. At night, he slept in the alley, squeezed under the overhanging eaves of the store to protect against the weather. He had an old sleeping bag and a shopping cart full of his earthly possessions.

Griff Slocum first appeared on Washington Street about five years ago, people said. He joined a small band of street people who hung out in the ravine at Turkey Neck, but there were tough guys down there, and Griff was afraid of them. He soon migrated out of Turkey Neck and made his home in the alleyways behind the stores.

Most of the merchants along Washington had chased Griff, but Hussam tolerated him. Hussam and his family had been driven from their homeland, and they had more sympathy for a man with nowhere to go. Griff tried to make himself as inconspicuous as possible, huddling in a small space, carefully putting any trash he made into the dumpster. And after a while, he and Mr. Hussam even greeted one another with a smile. It was the closest thing to a home that Griff Slocum had experienced.

Ernesto's good friend and fellow track member, Julio Avila, called Ernesto at six thirty.

"You know about Griff, huh, Ernie?" he asked.

"Yeah, too bad," Ernesto said. "Didn't your dad know him better than anybody? I used to see your dad treating him to a burger sometimes. They seemed to be talking. I couldn't hardly understand the guy,

13

but your dad seemed to be communicating with him okay."

Julio Avila's father was a down-and-outer too. The only reason he wasn't on the street like Griff Slocum was because he was the only parent of a son whom he loved dearly, Julio. Because Mr. Avila had Julio to live for and to think about, he did not fall as low as Griff Slocum, who seemed to have no family.

Mr. Avila would stir himself to look for a few odd jobs. Sometimes he collected cans early in the morning, even going to the trash cans on the curb and digging out the treasures. He would do anything he could to add to the meager family income. Julio and his father lived on Mr. Avila's disability pension from a back injury in the merchant marine, and on Julio's job as a cashier in the supermarket.

Now Julio said to Ernesto, "My pop knew him pretty well. Pop doesn't have a lot of what the rich folks call 'discretionary' money, but he'd always manage to get enough together to buy beer for himself and Griff. It kinda was the only social life Griff had. They'd talk, and Pop grew to be able to understand Griff's slurred speech. It meant so much to the guy to have a friend, at least one friend who treated him like a human being."

"Nice of your pop to have done that," Ernesto said. "Did Griff ever say anything about where he was from or what happened in his life to bring him down so low?"

"Yeah," Julio said. "Believe it or not, the guy was at UCLA. He dropped out when he was a sophomore. He had a car and a job. Then he started using. He got into drugs big-time. He went to jail for a five-year stretch one time. Got his jaw broken. Never healed right. That's why he talked funny. He came from a decent family, I guess. He even went to rehab to try to kick the stuff. It helped for a while, but then he went right back on. He used meth, cocaine, pain pills, anything he could get his hands on. He was on the skids and into free fall by the time he was thirty. He's thirty-eight … I mean he *was* thirty-eight."

"Thirty-eight!" Ernesto gasped. "That's *young!* He looked so much older. I thought he was like fifty or something. I wonder if he ever had any dreams?"

"Yeah, he loved baseball. He thought he'd be in the majors. That was when he was a kid," Julio said. "Then the drugs, they fried his brains, I guess. He'd stopped using three, four years ago, but it was too late. Maybe he had demons he couldn't handle, and that got him hooked, who knows? He didn't deserve to die by a dumpster in an alley with his head caved in. Lay there quite a while till they found him, bleeding out. It's not right, man," Julio's voice was rutted with sadness.

CHAPTER TWO

At school the next day, Ernesto ran into Carlos Negrete. He and Dom Reynosa used to be taggers in the *barrio* and dropouts from Cesar Chavez High. But Abel, Ernesto, and Luis Sandoval, Ernesto's father, "rescued" the boys and convinced them to return to school. Now they had painted a beautiful mural at the school, a work of art that was the pride of the school.

"Hey, Ernie," Carlos said, "I got something to tell you. Me and Dom were out late last night, and we saw something awful."

Ernesto wondered what Dom and Carlos were doing out late at night. He hoped they weren't up to their old bad habits, marking the *barrio* with graffiti. Some very dramatic graffiti had just appeared on the side of an abandoned warehouse on Polk Street— a dashing figure of Joaquin Murrieta, an outlaw once from California. It looked like the work of Carlos and Dom, but Ernesto didn't want to make any accusations. Still, it had created quite a stir in the neighborhood, and there was a difference of opinion over whether to paint it over or leave it.

"What did you guys see?" Ernesto asked.

"Me and Dom, we were just hanging out, you know, and we saw these guys taunting the old bum who died," Carlos said in a matter-of-fact voice that seemed to miss the extent of the horror he was describing.

"*What?*" Ernesto gasped.

"Yeah, it was like eleven o'clock or something, and there were like three guys with sticks, and they were like make-believe dueling with the old guy. And he was running this way and that. They were laughing like crazy," Carlos said.

"And you guys just watched and did

nothing?" Ernesto demanded. "You saw them harassing the poor guy, and you didn't do anything?"

"Oh no, man," Carlos said. "We stopped, and we ran them off. Me and Dom didn't have no weapons or anything, but you know the big wind we had a coupla days ago? Street was full of those palm fronds, and we grabbed them and whacked at the dudes and they ran. They were pretty drunk."

"Was Griff Slocum hurt or anything?" Ernesto asked.

"No. They didn't even touch him with the sticks. He was scared, though. He was glad when we run them off," Carlos said.

"Who were these guys, Carlos?" Ernesto asked. "Students at Chavez?"

"Yeah," Carlos said, "but remember, dude, I ain't telling you any of this. You never heard it from me. I'm no snitch. I don't tell on nobody. They ran off and got into a Toyota and took off. Rod Garcia was driving. I didn't recognize the other two. There was another guy in the car, but he was sleeping or something. Remember, Ernie, I never told you nothin', right?"

"I got it, homie," Ernesto said. "But just one thing. They didn't actually hit Griff Slocum, right?"

"Right. They were waving the sticks and laughing … like a make-believe bullfight. After we run them off, this guy Slocum just walked away. He wasn't hurt or nothin'. Dom, he asked the guy if he was okay. Slocum don't talk good, but he nodded and hurried away. Then he kinda stopped. He turned and looked at us. I think he said 'thanks' or something. I'm not sure."

"Thanks, Carlos," Ernesto said. "Oh, and by the way, there's an amazing mural on Joaquin Murrieta over on Polk, and it's pretty striking. You don't know anything about that, do you?"

Carlos smiled. "Don't know what you're talkin' about, man." He turned then and headed for class. Both Carlos and Dom were now seniors making decent grades and very likely to graduate.

Ernesto was disgusted by the story Carlos had told him, but he could imagine a drunken Rod Garcia acting that way. The guy had no class, and he often expressed a hatred of panhandlers. Ernesto thought that if Garcia and his friends were on Washington Street with Griff Slocum at eleven, they may have seen the person who killed Griff soon after.

At lunchtime, Ernesto walked over to where Rod and Clay and Mira Nuñez were eating. He didn't want to break his word to Carlos, so he looked directly at Rod Garcia and said, "Some lady in the *barrio* saw three dudes hanging around Griff Slocum last night shortly before he was killed. You were one of them, Garcia."

Rod Garcia turned pale. "That's a lie!" he screamed.

"She saw you and a couple of other guys harassing Griff, poking at him with sticks," Ernesto said coldly.

"Well, she's a liar," Rod stammered. "You trying to get me in trouble, Sandoval?"

21

"You guys were pretending Griff was a bull, and you were taunting him, and then some guys with palm fronds came and ran you off. That's what she saw, man. She recognized you, but she didn't know the others," Ernesto said. "I think you and your friends need to go to the police and tell them if you saw anybody else hanging around. You could have valuable information about the murder."

"The old witch who told you she saw me there was lying, Sandoval. You tell that old witch to stop telling lies about me. I was home last night studying."

Clay Aguirre had been silent to this point. He looked upset, though. "I was there at Rod's house. Mira was too. We were working on math problems till almost midnight," he said.

"Yeah, the boys were home all evening doing their homework," Mira added. "They never left Rod's house."

Carlos hadn't seen Clay Aguirre in the trio harassing Griff Slocum. He was probably in the car during the incident. But right now, he was willing to lie for Rod. He was lying for Rod, and Mira was backing him up.

"Well, in case you were there, dude, I'd go to the police and talk to them before they come and talk to you. If this lady saw you, then other people probably did too," Ernesto said.

"Hey, idiot," Rod almost shouted, "*I wasn't there!* What part of that don't you understand? If some old witch says she saw me, then maybe she needs new glasses!"

As Ernesto walked away, Clay, Rod, and Mira were in animated conversation. Ernesto couldn't hear what they were saying, but Mira Nuñez talked to Naomi later on. Though Ernesto and Clay were enemies, Naomi and Mira maintained a cordial relationship.

After school, Naomi told Ernesto that Mira had confided in her.

As Ernesto drove Naomi home, she said, "Mira is really worried, and Clay is just furious. Rod and Clay and two junior guys who're friends of Rod's were out drinking last night. Clay was sick. Rod pulled over on Washington. Clay tried to sleep it off before they drove on. While he was sleeping, the two juniors and Rod apparently spotted Griff Slocum stumbling around, and they thought they'd have some fun. They decided to harass him and play matador and bull or something," Naomi said with disgust.

"Carlos Negrete and Dom Reynosa came along and broke it up. Mira said Rod and the juniors were so drunk they were almost falling down. By the time they got back to Rod's car, Clay was coming around, but Rod drove home. Too bad a cop didn't pull him over. He would have gotten a DUI. Anyway, Clay didn't know anything about the incident until you told him that story of the witness, and now he could strangle Rod, but still, he's backing up the guy."

"Well, according to Carlos, the *bobos* didn't hurt Griff, and I don't think they had anything to do with what happened to him. Carlos said Griff was fine when the jerks drove away. I just hope I scared them enough that they go to the cops and give them any information they might have," Ernesto said.

Ernesto took a deep breath and headed home.

In the next few days, the results of the autopsy on Griff Slocum came out. He died of blunt force trauma to the head. The weapon, which was not found, was probably a pipe or poker. Because of an item found at the murder scene, the news reporter said the police were interviewing a person of interest.

The family of Rod Garcia contacted the most respected lawyer in the *barrio*, Arturo Sandoval, Luis Sandoval's brother, that day. Everyone in the *barrio* knew that no lawyer was better.

When police officers descended on the Garcia home, there were shock waves in the neighborhood. From something Rod Garcia's mother told a friend, the story quickly leaked. Rod Garcia's student body ID card was found in the vicinity of the murder scene. As he jumped around Griff Slocum wielding the stick and shouting, he had apparently dropped his wallet. He retrieved the wallet, but his ID card must have slipped out without him seeing or missing it.

"This is just unbelievable," Luis Sandoval said. "I have little respect for Rod Garcia or Clay Aguirre because of things they have done in the past, but I can't believe either boy was involved in what happened to poor Mr. Slocum. You told me, Ernie, that Rod and two other boys were harassing Griff, and he probably lost the ID card then. The boys were drunk. It easily could have slipped out."

"I told Rod to go to the police and admit to the ugly harassment. I didn't know he'd dropped his ID then, but it would've looked a lot better for him if he'd owned up to his stupid behavior before the police found the card," Ernesto said.

The Garcia family was in a state of shock during their son's interview. They knew nothing of what he and his friends had done, and they were repulsed. They were frightened too. A man had been murdered, and their son's ID was at the murder scene.

Rod admitted everything to the police. He identified the two juniors as Humberto Gomez and Rick Alanzar. Rod told the police that he and Rick and Humberto were drunk, and that it had seemed funny at the time to harass the bum, but they did him no harm. Rod swore that Griff Slocum had been alive and well when they left.

Police investigators called in Carlos Negrete and Dom Reynosa, and both boys told the same story that Rod had told. They described beating the drunken teenagers off with palm fronds, and they corroborated Rod Garcia's account that Griff Slocum was all right when the drunken boys drove away.

Later, the police interviewed Rick Alanzar and Humberto Gomez, and their story was the same as well.

No charges were pressed against Rod Garcia, but the police told him they may want to talk to him again.

At school the next day, Carlos Negrete approached Ernesto. "Dude, everything's coming up roses," he said. "Turns out those creeps, Rod and his friends, needed me and Dom to clear them of hurting the old home- less guy. When the cops found that idiot's ID card, they were hot on his trail. He had to admit what he and his friends had done, but he swore he never hurt the guy. If it hadn't been for me and Dom, he'd be in real hot water. When the cops found that ID, they thought they had their man. They had the handcuffs ready. It wouldn't bother me to see Garcia in the slammer, but I had to tell the truth. They left the guy standing and without a bruise."

"Then somebody else came along and

28

killed Griff Slocum," Ernesto said, shaking his head.

"Yeah, what a weird thing, dude. Slocum gets harassed by some drunken creeps, then he gets murdered by somebody else. I mean, it wasn't the guy's night, I guess. They say when your time comes, it comes." Carlos's expression changed then as a lighter mood took over. "I got good news, Ernie. You know that mural on Joaquin Murrieta on the side of the warehouse on Polk?"

"Yeah, the mural you know nothing about," Ernesto said wryly.

"Yeah, well … anyway, some dude liked it so much he took pictures of it. Came up on Tumblr. Some dude saw it, and he wants a mural on the side of his building now, and he wants to *pay* for it, man. In real money!" Carlos said.

"Oh, too bad it wasn't you guys who did the Murrieta painting," Ernesto said, laughing. Then he grabbed Carlos and gave him a hug. "I'm proud of you guys."

"Thanks, dude. We're gonna paint that

Padre Hidalgo who started the Mexican Revolution against Spain. We'll do a bang-up job," Carlos said. "Your dad never told us studying history could make us some cash."

In Mr. Davila's class the next day, Rod Garcia was very subdued. He knew he'd had a close call. Maybe it wasn't over yet. Until they had the person who killed Griff Slocum, Rod wasn't home free.

Everyone at Chavez High knew what had happened, and Rod Garcia felt humiliated. He didn't like Griff Slocum, but if he hadn't been stupidly drunk, he never would have harassed him like that. It was beyond stupid.

After school, Ernesto went over to Julio Avila's trailer where he lived with his father. Ernesto wanted to tell Mr. Avila that he had the right to be proud that he had brought some joy to the poor, lonely homeless man.

As Ernesto pulled into the driveway of

the trailer, he was surprised to see a VW bug already parked there. The Avilas did not usually have visitors. In fact, they did not let most people into their trailer.

Julio saw Ernesto pull up, and he swung open the door. "Come on in, homie," he said.

When Ernesto went inside the trailer, he saw a small white-haired lady sitting at the fold-down dinette.

Ernesto had never seen the woman before. She didn't look Hispanic. Julio cleared up Ernesto's puzzlement immediately. "Ernie, this is Griff Slocum's mother. Mrs. Slocum, this is Ernesto Sandoval, one of my buddies," he said.

Mr. Avila was sitting at the table opposite Mrs. Slocum. "She came all the way from San Francisco," he said.

The woman looked like she was past seventy, and her eyes were deep set and sorrowful. "Griff was my only child," she said.

"I'm really sorry, Mrs. Slocum," Ernesto

said. "I saw your son all the time. He was a nice man. He never bothered anybody. If you showed him a little kindness, he was so gracious and thankful."

A tear slipped down the woman's face. She looked fragile, like a glass goblet that could easily break. It was at that moment that Ernesto noticed the little box on her lap. It didn't look like an ordinary box. It looked like it contained something of value.

"I had my son cremated," Mrs. Slocum said. Her voice trembled for a moment, and then steadied itself. "These are his remains in the box. It's an ivory box. I'm taking him back to San Francisco, and he'll be interred with my husband, who died many years ago. Griff loved San Francisco. He liked to see the Giants play back in the day."

She cleared her throat then and said, "The reason I came here was to thank Mr. Avila in person. I have already been to the Iraqi man's store—Mr. Hussam. I thanked him. He allowed my son to stay there by his store where he felt safe. My son didn't contact me often, but he would sometimes write a letter. He always told me that he had one good friend who talked to him as if he were a normal person. A friend who would treat him to dinner and coffee when he could. That was you, Mr. Avila. And I want to thank you. Griff had said that when most people came in contact with him, they treated him as if he were garbage … but you treated him with respect."

Julio's father nodded. "I liked your son, Mrs. Slocum. He was a real person. There was nothing phony about him. He had this problem speaking, but we got to know each other well enough that I could understand him, and we had some nice conversations. He wanted to talk about baseball. I'm a baseball fan too, and we had good times talking about the old players who were so great."

Julio's father continued, "Life had batted him around, same as it's done for me. We both been in dark places, but Griff's was darker. I got this one big blessing that

Griff never had." He looked at his son. "This boy here. Without him, I'd be worse off than Griff was. So I don't judge him. I don't judge nobody."

Mrs. Slocum almost smiled. "When my son was a little boy, he'd sneak into the baseball park to watch the games. And he collected baseball cards. He was a good pitcher in Little League. He showed a lot of promise. But then he got into drugs. My husband and I tried to help him, but he started selling drugs. Went to prison. He came out a changed person. He'd been injured in prison, and he couldn't talk normally anymore. Griff was a kind boy, and he was so ashamed that he let his father and me down. That's why he didn't want to call us or write much. He was so ashamed of what had become of his life." She dabbed at her eyes with a handkerchief.

"Drugs are a terrible thing," Mr. Avila said. "I've done some, not the real hard stuff, but I know how terrible addiction can be."

"I wrote to Griff when his father died, but he didn't write back. I think it crushed him to know that his father had died without ever seeing him normal again. He had so much guilt. But, you know, even before the drugs, I always thought there was something wrong, but my husband and I didn't know how to deal with it," Mrs. Slocum said. She started to get up then. "Mr. Avila, thank you so much for bringing a little happiness into his life. Thank you." She grasped the man's hand. Then she tenderly picked up her little ivory box and held it close to her chest. She turned once more, this time to Julio. "Your father is a very nice man," she said.

"I know," Julio said. "I love him very much, ma'am, and thanks for taking the time to come here. *Vaya con dios.*"

CHAPTER THREE

When Ernesto Sandoval got home, he told his family about Griff Slocum's mother coming to see Mr. Avila. "His mom wanted to thank Julio's father for being kind to him," Ernesto said. "She said Griff was really into baseball. He collected baseball cards as a kid."

"Lot of us did that," Luis Sandoval said. "My dad treasured his cards. Traded some of them away, but he gave me some of his treasures. Roberto Clemente, for one."

"I got a few cards too," Ernesto said. "I got Derek Jeter."

Katalina, Ernesto's nine-year-old sister said, "I got a Sandy Koufax. It's all wrinkled. Was he important?"

"Yeah, he was great," Dad said.

"Some boy gave me a Dennis Kinney," Juanita, who was seven, said.

"I never heard of Dennis Kinney," Ernesto told his little sister.

"Sunday's the fiesta at Our Lady of Guadalupe Church you know, you guys," Maria Sandoval said. "Remember, we're all going around one o'clock. They've got games for the kids and face painting and all kinds of stuff, plus wonderful food."

Lena Sandoval, Ernesto's grandmother who lived with the family, smiled and said, "I'm making *tortilla española* like I do every year. People look forward to it. I'll be at the food booth with Conchita Ibarra. I make my tortillas the old way, and everybody expects them." A look of pride shone in her eyes.

"Good for you, Mama," Luis Sandoval said.

"They're raffling off a car this year," Mom said. "I bought ten tickets. Our car is getting a little creaky. It'd be something if we won the Jeep Patriot."

37

"You think we'll win, Mama?" Juanita asked.

Maria Sandoval laughed. "No, but I can dream, can't I? It was so nice of Mr. Carillo, the Jeep dealer, to donate the car. I know he's rich, but with the economy still hurting, it's difficult for people to give."

"Are we rich, Mama?" Juanita demanded.

This time, Luis Sandoval laughed. "No, *mi hija*, not in money but in blessings. In love and happiness. When I look at my beautiful *esposa*, my *muchachos* and *muchachas*, I feel like the richest man in the world," he said.

On Sunday, there was a huge crowd at the fiesta. Ernesto thought that just about everybody he knew was there. Along with the Jeep Patriot, other items were being raffled off, including a beautiful painting of Our Lady of Guadalupe. The painting was unusual in that the Virgin was appearing not only to Juan Diego, the young farmer, but to other young people, boys and girls who looked like teenagers from the *barrio* stood around her.

Padre Benito stood by the painting and said, "This was donated by two boys who are seniors at Cesar Chavez High School. They made this painting for the fiesta and gave it to us. Isn't it remarkable? Look how radiant the Virgin is, and how happy she is to see so many boys and girls. It is a masterpiece!"

"Oh, I want that for my mom's birthday," Carmen Ibarra cried. "I bought thirty tickets. Mom would just love that in the den. The Virgin looks just like *us!*"

Paul Morales was at Carmen's side and he said, "Babe, I bought some tickets too, and if I win, it's yours."

"See how nice he is?" Carmen giggled. "Even if he does have a rattlesnake tattooed on his hand!"

Ernesto, Julio, Mona, Naomi, and Carmen were in line for fish tacos when loud, angry voices exploded from the church parking lot.

Padre Benito looked alarmed. "Oh," he groaned. "One year a fight broke out and a boy was stabbed!"

Ernesto shouted to Abel and Paul, "We gotta go check the parking lot, dudes. Trouble out there."

Ernesto, Abel, Paul, and Julio ran to the parking lot. They were all big, muscular boys who could handle pretty much anything. They were likely to intimidate whoever was yelling.

As they approached the parking lot, Ernesto recognized Clay's voice. He had the shrillest voice Ernesto ever heard. "You idiot! What kind of a fool drops his ID right where he's hassling some old bum?"

"I was drunk," Rod Garcia said. "You were drunk too, man!"

"Yeah, but I had the sense to stay in the car and try to sleep it off, man. You and those psycho friends of yours had to look for trouble. You and Gomez and Alanzar had to hassle that bum. You're morons!" Clay snarled. "And you made trouble for me. I was called into Ms. Sanchez's office, and she lectured me about underage drinking and being mixed up with dudes who'd pull such a rotten stunt. She told me I could be kicked off the football team because of you idiots!"

"They won't kick you off," Rod said. "We didn't even do anything. We didn't touch the bum. We just kinda waved our sticks at him. We were having fun. Sanchez talked to me and the other guys too, but she didn't say we'd be suspended or anything. She just gave us a warning not to step over the line again."

"And then the dude gets murdered the same night," Clay ranted. "What do you think all this does to my reputation? People think I was mixed up in something horrible—I slept through the whole thing!"

Ernesto led the way into the parking lot with the other three behind him. "You guys," Ernesto said, "keep it down. You're scaring people over at the fiesta." Paul, Abel, and Julio stood behind Ernesto, looking menacing.

"I didn't do anything wrong," Clay yelled. "This fool here and his creepy junior friends started it all. Why do you have to hang out with junior punks anyway?"

"Humberto Gomez is my cousin," Rod Garcia said. "Rick Alanzar is his best friend."

Clay Aguirre was strident and angry, but Rod Garcia seemed subdued. Rod turned to Ernesto and spoke almost apologetically. "We were drunk, and old Slocum was staggering around, and we just on the spur of the moment picked up sticks and pretended he was a bull and we were matadors. We were just kidding around. Nobody woulda got hurt."

"Well," Ernesto said, "stop yelling over here. You're scaring the women and kids. This is a fiesta for kids and families. If you guys got a beef, take it somewhere else, okay?" With that, Ernesto and the others returned to the fiesta.

When Ernesto and his friends were gone, Clay turned to Rod and said bitterly,

42

"You see what you've done, fool? You've given that jackass Sandoval the chance to lecture us like we're punks."

When Ernesto returned to the fiesta, he took another look at the painting of Our Lady of Guadalupe. He smiled to read the name "Cardom" scrawled on the bottom. Carlos Negrete and Dom Reynosa. The minute he saw the painting with its raw, natural beauty, he knew it was theirs.

Ernesto and his friends then sat down to eat their fish tacos and drink their sodas. "Man, these fish tacos are good," Ernesto said. "They're as good as you make, Abel."

Abel smiled.

"You made the fish tacos for this booth, didn't you?" Ernesto cried.

"Could be," Abel said. He planned to enter culinary school once he graduated from Chavez. He was growing more skilled by the day because he worked part time at an upscale eatery, the Sting Ray.

Julio told everybody about Mrs. Slocum coming to their house then. "The poor lady appreciated the fact that Pop treated her son like a human being. She told us a lot of stuff about him that we never knew. He wanted to play professional baseball, but the drugs got in the way. And since he was a kid, he collected baseball cards. I guess he traded them all away for drugs."

Abel shook his head. "Too bad. Some of those baseball cards get really valuable. Griff coulda used some cash," he said.

"Yeah," Paul Morales said. "It was on the Internet the other day that some old person left a baseball card to some charity, and when they went to turn it in, it was worth several hundred thousand dollars. It blew them away."

"Wow," Mona said. "Whose card would be that valuable? My grandfather used to talk about Babe Ruth. Was it his card?"

"No," Paul said. "It was a Honus Wagner."

"Who?" Carmen asked. "I never heard of him."

"Yeah," Paul said. "He was the first guy

44

to get into the Baseball Hall of Fame when they started that place in the 1930s. Wagner made like three thousand four hundred hits or something."

"Is that good?" Naomi asked.

"Well, yeah," Julio said. "It's way better than some of the guys who came along later. Like Tony Gwynn, he got a little over three thousand hits, and he's one of the all-time greats, but Wagner made four hundred more."

"The guy on the Internet said a Honus Wagner card, even in fair condition, is worth a fortune," Paul said.

"Poor Griff Slocum," Naomi said. "If he was really into collecting baseball cards, and if he'd saved them, that might have been a way off the streets."

"He wasn't a very lucky guy, I guess," Julio said. "Probably owned a bunch of baseball cards featuring stiffs who never even made it to the World Series."

"I'll say he wasn't lucky," Mona said sadly. "Think about what happened to the poor guy in *one night!* First he gets hassled by some mean punks, and then he gets murdered by somebody else. I mean, is that terrible or what?"

"You know," Julio said, "I got a suspicious mind. I'm not denying that, but I don't believe in coincidences. I can't believe that the murder and the hassling by those creeps was totally disconnected. I've got no idea how they fit together, but it's just too much to swallow that at eleven o'clock he's getting tormented by those three punks, and he's dead an hour later."

"So," Ernesto said, "you think one of those guys who was hassling him came back and killed him? Dude, that makes no sense. They're creeps, but they're not criminals. Why would they do a thing like that?"

"Yeah," Naomi said. "I know Rod Garcia is a jerk, and I've talked to that Humberto a few times, and he's a jerk too. But I just can't wrap my head around the idea that one of those boys beat poor Griff Slocum to death."

"And why?" Abel said. "Maybe the poor guy said some bad words to them while they were hassling him, though I doubt it. Griff was as meek a human being as I've ever seen, even more of a wimp than my father, who's a class-A wimp. But even if he'd said something, it couldn't have made them mad enough to come back and kill the dude."

"It's all so horrible," Naomi said. "It makes my skin crawl to think a student at Cesar Chavez High could have killed a helpless man in cold blood."

Julio looked over at Mona, his girl-friend. He and Mona had been dating just a short time. Julio had a hard time convincing her parents to let him date their precious only daughter. Julio struck the Corsellas as a tough, even dangerous street kid, and in many ways he was. He sometimes carried a switchblade to use for self-defense if he had to.

When Julio and his father had been homeless, they had camped in the ravine—in

47

Turkey Neck, a homeless camp for all kinds of men. Most were poor souls wasted by life, and some were runaway kids, but a few were bad to the bone, and you needed a switchblade to fight off a dude who would cut your throat for five dollars.

"Naomi, I know it's hard to think of a kid going to classes at Chavez turning into a murderer, but you never know. We don't know what evil lurks in people. We don't even know sometimes what kind of evil lurks in our own souls."

"I hope the police find the guy who did it," Mona said. "I hope they find him and put him in jail for the rest of his life. Griff Slocum never hurt anybody. He didn't deserve to end up like that."

"I know Rod and Humberto a little, but does anybody know this Rick Alanzar?" Naomi asked.

Paul Morales grinned. "It's always easier to think it was some dude we don't know, somebody we've never had a burrito with. The stranger out there. He's the one who did it," Paul said in a sarcastic voice.

Naomi looked at Paul, "Do *you* know Rick?"

"He's come in the electronics store a few times to buy stuff. He looks like an ordinary guy, Naomi. No hair growing out of his ears, no red glow to his eyes," Paul said.

Naomi looked at Carmen. "Carmen, your boyfriend is making fun of me," she complained, half smiling.

Carmen laughed. "That's Paul. He does it to me all the time."

That evening was the raffle for the Jeep Patriot and the *Our Lady of Guadalupe* painting, plus some smaller items like gift baskets full of wine, cheese, and gourmet chocolates.

A family nobody knew, who had bought a few tickets at the fiesta just to help the poor little church with the leaky roof, won the Jeep Patriot.

Carmen Ibarra won the painting because she had told everyone she wanted it as a gift for her mother. And because Carmen was so well loved, as was Conchita Ibarra, Carmen's mother, most people, not just Ernesto, had bought tickets in Carmen's name.

Everyone had a great time at the fiesta, and the church had raised enough money to fix their roof. They also raised enough to keep the outreach to the poor going for another year, including distributing food to needy families twice a week.

That night, Ernesto Sandoval had trouble sleeping. He kept thinking about what Julio had said, that there was some connection between the three boys who had hassled Griff Slocum and his murder just hours later. Ernesto hated to admit it, but he agreed with Julio. He didn't much believe in coincidences either.

Ernesto knew and disliked Rod Garcia, but he was pretty sure the guy wasn't a murderer. Ernesto had lost respect for

Humberto Gomez, Rod's cousin, when he saw him bullying kids at school. He was a tough, mean kid. Though Ernesto had never talked to Rick Alanzar, he thought he seemed like a quiet loner. Whenever some crime was committed, they often said the culprit was a loner.

But Ernesto just couldn't imagine any of the three harming Griff Slocum.

What if one of the guys had spotted something of value on Griff? As they hassled him, maybe he dropped a wad of money he had stashed. Some homeless people had quite a sum.

Maybe Griff quickly retrieved the money, and one of the three came back alone for it. Maybe the person thought he'd be sleeping, and they could just roll a drunk. Maybe Griff fought for his money.

CHAPTER FOUR

Although they gave no specific details, the police released a statement the following day that Griff Slocum was in possession of a valuable item on the night he had been murdered. On his body had been found a handwritten will directing the item to be sent to his mother upon his death, though neither she nor anyone else knew of its existence.

The item had been stolen, undoubtedly by the person who had murdered him.

Everybody at Cesar Chavez High speculated about the item at lunch the next day. Some thought he had owned a diamond ring, maybe from some lost relationship. Some thought it might have been a fine watch. With a glint in his eye, Julio Avila said, "He was crazy about baseball cards. His mom said he traded 'em all away for drugs. But maybe not. Maybe he kept one. Maybe he kept the best one."

There were not enough streetlights on Washington. The local business people were always pleading for better lighting. They had gone to the city council before Emilio Zapata Ibarra was on the council, and the local councilman, Monte Esposito, said it was not a first priority. Now since the murder of Griff Slocum, the chorus of demands for better lighting increased.

The city council was taking up the matter on Monday afternoon, and Ernesto and Naomi went down to listen. As they walked into the council chambers, they spotted some of the businesspeople, including Mr. Hussam who sat in front beside the lady who ran the thrift store.

"We have two businesspeople with us this afternoon," Mr. Ibarra began the session. "The tragic murder of Mr. Griff Slocum occurred on Washington Street, close to their places of business."

Mr. Hussam seemed very nervous as he spoke. In the country where he came from, it was very dangerous to confront the authorities with a complaint. Men had been found dead in alleys for doing less than that. But Mr. Hussam had known Griff Slocum for quite some time and knew he was a decent man who deserved better than having his head caved in on a dark street.

"Ladies and gentlemen of the council," Mr. Hussam said, "I think if Washington Street had more streetlights, there would be less crime. Criminals like to work in the dark. I do not know if the boys who tormented Mr. Slocum on the night he died had anything to do with his murder, but I do not think those boys would have done such a thing on a well-lit street where passing cars would have seen the evil act. I have seen gang members on the street at night, and it is dangerous for pedestrians to walk there. I am asking you to put in more street-lights for everybody's sake, maybe in honor of Mr. Slocum who died in the darkness."

Applause swept the room, and Mr. Hussam smiled and made a small bow before hurrying back to his seat.

Miriam Ocasa, who ran the thrift store, spoke then. "I work late at night on my inventory, and I'm scared to even walk to my car in that dark spot. Now I look at where the poor man died, and there is no light at all. There are lights about fifteen feet away, but whoever killed the poor man was able to do his deed in the dark, and I hope we do something about that today."

Applause followed Ms. Ocasa's comments as well, and then the council took up the issue.

One of the councilmen said, "Of course, I would like to add more streetlights, but I would also like to keep the libraries open longer. I would like to repair more potholes. We cannot do everything, and streetlights are not the most important project."

A councilwoman stood to say, "I think we should commission a study of this problem and ask the members of the commission to get back to us when they can."

Ernesto groaned and looked at Naomi. "A favorite stalling tactic," he mumbled. "Pass the buck to some commission and maybe people will forget about it."

One of Councilman Ibarra's aides, David Morales, leaned over to talk to the councilman. David Morales was Paul Morales's brother, and he had been in prison for two years. When he got out, he couldn't find a job. In a gesture of kindness that blew David and his brother away, Mr. Ibarra hired him. Now David Morales was Mr. Ibarra's best aide. He was on top of every issue, and he had every fact at the tips of his fingers. He was able to deal with angry constituents and send them away happy.

David Morales now handed Mr. Ibarra a folder. It was the result of the research on the problem that David had done.

Mr. Ibarra addressed the council after scanning the folder. "My aide, Mr. Morales, has given me statistics to the effect that street crime declines as much as forty percent when streets are well-lit. In some cases, the decline is even higher. And this is for all kinds of crime: mugging, assault, robbery. Mr. Morales has discovered that Washington Street is well-lit in most areas, but the space between lights is noticeably wider in this particular area."

Mr. Ibarra pressed on. "The twenty-four-seven store Mr. Hussam owns and the thrift store Ms. Ocasa owns occupy the darkest areas of the street. I believe these businesses have been neglected owing to the type of clientele, poorer people. I am therefore offering to vote for a motion to immediately remedy this injustice by installing appropriate streetlights that will illuminate the area." Mr. Ibarra paused.

"It is too late to save Mr. Slocum. I cannot say if more lighting would have dissuaded those wicked boys from harassing the man, or if it might have prevented the murder, but if there had been good lighting, a life might have been saved. So in honor of the poor soul who, as Mr. Hussam said, died in the darkness, I urge an affirmative vote," Carmen's father concluded.

"He's good," Ernesto whispered to Naomi. "Man, he's good."

Naomi smiled. "Yeah, he's quite an orator," she said.

When the city council voted, only two people voted against the new lights. The motion passed to loud applause.

Mr. Ibarra turned to David and patted him on the shoulder. He had once more done the research and given Mr. Ibarra the ammunition to run with the motion.

After the city council had adjourned, David Morales and a close friend from the office, Livy Majors, met Ernesto and Naomi for lunch. David and Livy were dating now, and Ernesto was really happy for both of them. In spite of the fact that he'd broken into stores and served two years in prison,

David Morales was at heart a good person. He had accepted responsibility for what he'd done. He made no excuses and turned his life around.

"Mr. Ibarra was great, wasn't he?" David said. "I'm so proud to work for him. He's done more for the people in the *barrio* than all his predecessors put together."

"With this dude's help," Livy said, squeezing David's hand and smiling at him.

"I'm glad a light is going on in that dark spot where poor Mr. Slocum died," Naomi said. "Everybody is wondering what Mr. Slocum had that somebody would kill him for. I'm hearing all kinds of rumors."

"Yeah," David said. "Apparently it was worth an incredible amount of money. To think that a man who seemed destitute was carrying around something so valuable."

"David, you know Julio Avila, my friend?" Ernesto asked.

"Sure, I've met him. Quite a runner," David said. "And I understand his father befriended Mr. Slocum."

"Yeah, well, Julio has a theory that the valuable item Mr. Slocum was killed for was a baseball card. You know Mr. Slocum was a baseball card collector, but I guess he traded most of them away, but Julio thinks he kept a really rare one."

"The only card I can think of that'd be worth what they seem to be hinting at is a Honus Wagner," David said.

"Wouldn't it be unbelievable if Griff had a Honus Wagner?" Ernesto asked. "There he was, living on the street, and he could have sold the card and had a decent life."

David's expression grew serious. "Maybe if it was a card, it became more than that to him. Maybe it stood for all the lost dreams. Maybe it connected him to the man he wanted to be."

"If it was a baseball card, the cops know it, and if the murderer tries to sell it, won't he get caught?" Ernesto asked as he finished his BLT.

"Well, I unfortunately know a little

bit about that," David said. "When Augie and I would steal stuff, Augie had some really sophisticated fences who'd take hot stuff. Some collector might want a Honus Wagner so bad he'd trade for a hot one under the table, even one with blood on it."

Ernesto shook his head. "To kill a guy like that. It's so sick. Poor Griff probably fought for it. It would have been like parting with the only good thing he had."

"You know what," Naomi said. "Carmen and I were just walking down Washington Street that really hot day we had last August. It must have been a hundred in the shade. We'd just bought some *paletas* and were enjoying them. We passed Griff and he stared at our *paletas*, and he had such a longing in his eyes. We turned around and got one for him. He was so happy. I remember it was grape. Then I noticed something I'd never seen before. His shirt was way open because of the heat, and I saw he had a chain around his neck and a sort of little leather pouch attached to the chain, like what was inside was important. I wonder if—"

"Those guys who were coming at him with sticks and making him jump around in fear," Ernesto said. "They might have seen the pouch on the chain too. One of them maybe came back to check out what was so important to Griff Slocum that he kept it in a pouch like that."

Livy Majors looked very sad. "That could've been. The man was weak and wasted. Whoever came to take what he had probably thought he'd give it up without a fight, but he probably found strength he never thought he had, and the only way they could get the thing was to, you know, put him down. Whatever it was, a baseball card or whatever, it was something to die for. That's what he must have thought anyway."

"Ernie," David said, "you know that guy Rod Garcia pretty well. I know you don't like him, but do you think he'd have it in him to do something so monstrous?"

"No," Ernesto said, "but then I'm no judge, man. Clay Aguirre is always accusing me of having a soft spot in my heart for guys who aren't any good. I think I always give somebody the benefit of the doubt."

"The other two guys who were with Garcia," David said, "you know them?"

"Rod's cousin, Humberto, he's a bully, but nothing to raise the red flag. I don't know Rick at all. I have to believe some other guy came along and, you know, took advantage of the situation," Ernesto said.

David nodded. "When I was in prison, I got to know a lot of guys who did awful things. Most of them, you know, were pretty ordinary, like the guys you meet every day. Sometimes something just snaps—jealousy, greed, lust. I know I was in a really dark place in prison. I'd given up hope. If it hadn't been for Paul being so faithful, coming to see me every chance he got. I didn't even care that he was yelling at me and calling me names. *He was there*. He loved me in spite of everything. He's such a good guy. I owe him everything," David said.

Ernesto went over to see Abel Ruiz after school the next day. Abel was not as good a student as Ernesto, and he was hung up on a science project. Ernesto worked with him for two hours and got it done. Then he headed home.

Penelope Ruiz, Abel's fourteen-year-old sister and a freshman at Chavez, had stayed at school late for music lessons, and she came home on her bike. Her mother was allowing that again after several months of insisting that Penelope be picked up and driven home. Penelope had seemed to mature quite a bit.

"Hey, Penny," Ernesto greeted her. She was cute, if a tiny bit overweight. She loved candies and cookies.

"Hey, Ernie," Penny said, slamming down her books. "What a freakin' bad day I had!"

"What's up?" Abel asked.

"Oh, Abel, me and you, we're losers. We lost out in the DNA department. Tomás got all the good stuff. Our brother is charming, cute, smart, with lots of girlfriends. You got dumped by Claudia, and me, I can't even *get* a boyfriend!" Penelope raved.

"You're only fourteen," Ernesto said. "There's plenty of time for boyfriends when you're older."

"You sound just like Mom," Penelope exploded.

Liza Ruiz had been showering, but now she came out, wrapped in a terry cloth robe, a towel turban on her head. "What did you say, young lady?" she demanded.

"Nothing," Penelope said. "It's just that I hate school so much. Bratty kids and boring teachers. Every single girl in the freshman class has a boyfriend except me. Everybody hates me, especially the boys."

"Penelope Ruiz," Mom scolded, "will you stop that! When I was your age, I was still playing with my Barbie dolls, and the closest thing I had to a boyfriend was Ken!"

65

Penelope collapsed on the couch, clutching her head. "Oh my gosh, that's so ridiculous I think I'm gonna barf! I should play with dolls?" she cried. She jumped up and went to the end table where there were two small ivory dancers. Penelope clutched them and said, "Hello, Igor, meet Babette!"

"Stop it," Mom snarled. She looked at Ernesto. "Isn't she terrible? I'm really mortified. Your sisters are nice and sweet, aren't they, Ernie? Not like Penny."

"Well, Katalina is only nine, and she's already ditched her teddy bear," Ernesto said.

"I want a boyfriend," Penelope wailed. "I don't mean a hot romance. I just want a guy who's nice to me and maybe holds my hand once in a while. That witchy Lacey Serrano, she's got the coolest boyfriend. He's a junior! And he buys her beautiful things, not trinkets. He got her an awesome necklace from Osterman's Jewelry Store."

"A junior dude dating a freshman?" Ernesto asked frowning. "Not good."

"So what?" Penelope yelled. "I'm almost fifteen, and the juniors are sixteen. What's the big deal? Berto Gomez is soooo handsome. That nasty Lacey doesn't deserve a cute jock like him."

"Humberto Gomez?" Ernesto repeated the name. "Little Lacey Serrano is dating him?"

"She's not little," Penelope scoffed. "You should see her. She's huge. She wears her mother's stuff. She thinks she's the hottest thing in the whole school. She stands there and waits for Berto after school, and he picks her up in his car and kisses her!"

"She's a creep," Ernesto said grimly. "Before Ms. Sanchez got after her, she'd taunt poor Angel Roma and her sick grandmother when they'd go for a walk."

"I don't care," Penelope said. "All I know is she's got a great boyfriend and I don't!"

"Penelope," Ernesto said rather sternly, "Humberto Gomez is a creep too. He got stoned the other night, and he and

67

his buddies were tormenting poor Griff Slocum, pretending he was a bull and they were matadors. I'm shocked that Lacey's mother lets Lacey go around with somebody like that."

Abel had been silent, but now he turned to his sister. "Penny, don't be so anxious for a boyfriend. I wanted a girlfriend real bad, and Claudia Villa made me really happy, but then she dumped me, and it wasn't worth it. I'm seventeen, and the next time I get involved with a girl, I'm gonna be much, much older. I'm doing fine by myself," he said.

Penny looked at her brother. They didn't always get along, but generally he was a decent brother. Penelope never doubted that Abel really did love her. "But, Abel, you don't understand. Every girl in the freshman class is talking about their boyfriends, and I feel like a freak!"

Ernesto wasn't thinking about the argument going on between Penelope and her family. He was thinking about Humberto

Gomez. There were few boys in the *barrio* with enough money to buy jewelry at Osterman's. You couldn't get out of there without spending at least a couple hundred. The Gomez family was lower middle class.

"Penelope," Ernesto said, "how do you know this Gomez dude got Lacey something expensive from Osterman's?"

"Oh, she brags all the time, the little witch," Penelope said bitterly. "I'd like to wrap that necklace around her neck and tighten it."

"But how do you know it's not some cheapie necklace from the drugstore and Gomez just wanted to act big so he told her it was from Osterman's?" Ernesto pressed.

Penelope rolled her eyes. "She showed me the sales slip, dumbo! It cost a hundred and eighty dollars!" she said.

"Don't call my homie 'dumbo,' Penny," Abel said.

Ernesto's head was spinning. Humberto Gomez had enough money to get a little twit like Lacey a necklace for a hundred and eighty dollars? He drove a beater and sometimes came to school without lunch. Was Humberto already reaping the rewards of the crime that left Griff Slocum dead by a dumpster in the alley on Washington?

CHAPTER FIVE

When Rod Garcia was leaving school the next day, Ernesto Sandoval confronted him. "I need to talk to you, man," Ernesto said.

Ordinarily, Rod would have blown him off, but since the incident the night Griff died, he was subdued. "Yeah, what's up?" he said.

"Something's bothering me, man," Ernesto said. "You know about the talk that Griff Slocum had something real valuable on him the night he was killed. Some guys are even saying he might have had some valuable baseball card. Well, your cousin and Rick and you were hassling him that night and—"

"Yeah," Rod said ruefully. "We picked

71

a heckuva time to get drunk and play stupid games with an old hobo. Who woulda thought somebody else would come along and murder him the same night! I've thought about it a lot. Maybe some guy was standing in the shadows, and when he saw how weak and confused Slocum was, he thought he'd make a good victim."

"Rod, I don't know your cousin, Humberto Gomez, except that he doesn't come from money. He's been at school a few times trying to bum a lunch off somebody else 'cause he said his parents were hard up. Well, he just went down to Osterman's and bought a necklace for some freshman here at Chavez for almost two hundred bucks," Ernesto said.

Rod Garcia stood there, shock spreading over his features. "You're trying to screw my cousin, aren't you, Sandoval? You're playing detective, and you think you can nail Humberto. You're not willing to let the cops do the investigating. I'm telling you, Sandoval, Clay is right.

You got the biggest ego on the planet. You think you can run the world. Well, let me tell you something—Humberto makes a lot of money on tips when he works at the car wash 'cause he does a great job. Just because he bought a gift for a chick doesn't mean—I can't believe you, man! You're practically accusing my cousin of killing the old bum for his stuff. Maybe you think Rick and I were in on it too," Rod Garcia's voice throbbed with emotion.

"I'm not accusing anybody," Ernesto said.

"Yes you are," Rod cried. "It's all over that smug face of yours. Well, let me tell you something, Sandoval. Humberto is a great guy. He's my mom's brother's kid. He's got good parents, and he's never been in trouble before. He's not like those dirty wanna-be gangbangers you hang out with. Hey, you know what *I* think happened? I think Reynosa or Negrete doubled back and robbed and killed the old bum. Yeah, when they were fighting with us, they spied

73

something valuable, chased us off, and then came back. One of them, or both of them, did in the old fool. So, you watch yourself, Sandoval, you tell lies about my cousin, and I'm gonna tell the cops what I think happened, okay?"

Ernesto turned and walked to his Volvo. Unfortunately, Garcia had a point. Ernesto was sure in his own heart that Dom and Carlos would never harm anybody, but they *were* on the scene, just as Garcia, Gomez, and Alanzar were. Maybe, while the five boys were going at each other, Griff Slocum reached for that leather packet on the chain to make sure his treasure was safe, and one of them noticed the gesture. Ernesto knew it couldn't have been Dom or Carlos, but the police didn't know those boys like Ernesto did.

Ernesto went over to the warehouse on Polk Street where Carlos and Dom were working on their mural of Padre Hidalgo. The boys had studied various paintings of the man, and they had chosen to portray him wearing a dark cassock, with a scroll in his hand and a look of determination on his bearded face. With his followers behind him, he was issuing the *Grito de Dolores,* the cry demanding Mexico's freedom from Spain. It was September 16, 1810, the day forever after celebrated as Mexican Independence Day.

"Looking good, guys," Ernesto shouted.

Carlos grinned. "Thanks, homie," he said.

"Some gig, huh, man?" Dom said. "We're getting like those big-shot muralists you told us about a long time ago."

When Carlos and Dom stopped for lunch, Ernesto joined them. They all bought chicken tacos at a nearby little Mexican eatery.

"You know, dudes," Ernesto said. "I keep thinking about poor Griff Slocum. Word is he had something valuable, and he died fighting for it."

"Yeah," Carlos said. "When we were driving those dudes off with the palm fronds, and Griff was bobbing and weaving to avoid them, I saw a chain around his neck. He had some sort of leather thing held by the chain. I figured it was a little wallet where he kept a few bucks."

"But I guess it was something more valuable, huh?" Dom asked. "Some guys are saying it was maybe some valuable baseball card."

"Do you think it could have partially fallen out or something and gotten the attention of somebody?" Ernesto asked.

"Nah," Carlos said. "It was real dark. Only thing is, Griff had his right hand on the leather pouch the whole time, like he didn't want to lose that. I sorta thought it was maybe a religious medal that he didn't want to lose. A medal from his mother or something. I know my *abuela* has this medal of the Virgin on a chain, and when she's walking, she's always got her hand over it, so it doesn't fall and get lost."

"A lot of homeless guys keep a little stash of money in pouches on a chain or tied to their underwear," Dom said. "I never dreamed Griff had anything real valuable."

"Maybe it looked to those other three guys that he was protecting something valuable," Ernesto said.

"Maybe," Dom said, "but they were so drunk, man. I mean, when we whipped them off with the palm fronds, they took off running."

"Yeah," Carlos said. "I don't think those dudes had enough sense to figure out anything."

"The thing that got me wondering was that one of them, Humberto Gomez, he's given an expensive jewelry gift to his freshman girlfriend. All the time I've known the guy, he's been hurting for money, but now he's suddenly spending big. I told Rod Garcia, his cousin, and the guy went ballistic. He claims Humberto made the money for the necklace working at the car wash and making big tips, but I haven't seen him there since last summer. I think they fired him," Ernesto said.

"Yeah, that sounds suspicious," Dom said. "Hey, maybe Humberto happened to see the guy who did the crime and the guy is paying him off, you know?"

Ernesto nodded. The truth was he never thought of that, but it made sense.

On Sunday, Ernesto, Naomi, and Abel planned to do something for their ninth graders in the mentoring program. Ernesto had set that up when he became senior class president. The student Ernesto mentored was Richie Loranzo, who lived in a foster home after his father shot his mother. Naomi mentored Angel Roma, who was from a single-parent home with a disabled grandmother. Abel mentored Bobby Padilla, also from a single-parent home. Bobby had run away from his mother once when she threatened to send him to live with his father.

Ernesto borrowed Cruz Lopez's wildly painted van for the trip to a tide-pooling and beachcombing expedition. The van had room for everybody, and the freshmen loved it.

Abel and Naomi had packed delicious sandwiches and apple pie, and Ernesto brought sodas.

"We like your sister, Penelope," Angel told Abel as they drove. "She's pretty cool."

Abel made a face and said, "Good." The Ruiz family had been in turmoil lately with Penelope expressing her hatred of school and everything about it.

"Penny eats lunch with us every day," Richie Loranzo said. "I guess she wants a boyfriend. I like her, but I don't want to be her boyfriend 'cause I like somebody else."

Ernesto noticed that Angel Roma giggled and turned red. Ernesto figured she must be the girl Richie liked.

Bobby Padilla said, "Girls are needy. I don't want a girlfriend."

Angel giggled again and looked at Richie who turned red too.

"When the tide's low like it is today,"

Naomi said, "you get to see such interesting stuff. I came here the first time when I was about six, and I was blown away."

They parked the van in a large parking lot between two grassy areas. Because Ernesto had been driving the van, the ninth graders assumed it was his.

"Ernie," Richie asked, "why did you paint all the monsters and stuff on your van?"

"Yeah," Bobby said. "And the different-colored snakes. I like them."

"It's not my van," Ernesto said. "The dude who owns it is Cruz Lopez, and he likes to paint wild stuff on his van."

Everybody had been instructed to wear good walking shoes, and they hiked single file across a sandy beach.

"What're all those big buildings up there?" Angel asked.

"That's a college where the scientists study the ocean," Ernesto said.

"I'd like to study the ocean," Angel said. "I love the ocean."

"Maybe you will study the ocean some-day," Naomi said.

"Yeah," Ernesto said. "You might be in one of those big buildings working as a scientist."

Angel Roma smiled happily.

They walked under a pier, and the cliffs to their right got steeper. "Careful now," Abel cautioned. "We'll be walking on slippery rocks."

"There's the tide pool," Ernesto said.

"Wow," Richie said, "everything is wiggling."

"Plants and animals," Ernesto said.

"I think I see an octopus," Richie cried. "Can I have him for a pet?"

"You can't take anything from here," Ernesto said. "Everything is protected. You can look and take pictures."

"An octopus would be a bad pet anyway," Abel said. "He'd grab at you with all his arms."

There were tiny fish and sea stars in the water.

"What's that?" Bobby asked. "What's that thing crawling out of the shell?"

"That's a hermit crab," Abel said. "He lives in the shell sometimes. It's like his second home."

They walked on to where a finger of gray rock reached out into the ocean. "That's volcanic rock," Ernesto said. "This is the only volcanic rock on the whole coastline. It's really old. Stuff from the middle of the earth pushed up and formed that finger about eleven million years ago."

"Who was living here then?" Angel asked. "We're studying California history now, about the Hupa and the Yurok Indians. Did they see the ground push up?"

"No," Ernesto said. "That happened before there were people on the planet."

They walked to a sandy beach and laid down blankets to sit on. Abel and Naomi brought the picnic baskets, and Ernesto brought the drinks. Abel produced ham and cheese tortilla wraps with cheddar cheese, sour cream, whole kernel corn, and red and green peppers. He brought the ingredients in a small ice chest so he could make everything fresh. Each wrap had a slice of ham with cilantro sprigs.

"These are so good," Angel said.

"Well," Naomi said, "I helped Abel shop for the stuff and helped pack the baskets, and I made the apple pies."

"Are you really a chef, Abel?" Richie asked. "How could you be a chef? You're just a kid. Aren't chefs old men?"

"Who told you I was a chef?" Abel asked.

"Penelope did. She said she had a really cool brother who could cook better than anybody, and that someday he was gonna be famous all over the world and stuff," Richie said.

Abel smiled. He looked touched. "Penny doesn't say stuff like that to me," he said.

"Your sister is jealous of old Lacey Serrano," Angel told Abel. Angel recalled how she and her grandmother would walk down the street and how Lacey and her friends would walk behind them, making fun of them because Grandma was unsteady on her feet. Angel's grandmother had Parkinson's disease, and she needed exercise, but Lacey's cruelty made everything harder.

"I hate Lacey," Richie said. "She's mean to everybody except her old boyfriend. She's all gooey around him."

"He's weird," Bobby Padilla added. "He's a junior, and he wants to be with a freshman. Lacey is bigger than most of the freshmen girls, but she's still only a freshman. We call her boyfriend Dumberto, but his real name is Humberto. Lacey calls him Berto."

Richie, Angel, and Bobby joined in derisive laughter. "Dumberto, Dumberto," they chanted, laughing until they cried.

"Guys, that's not really nice. You should be an example and not call people names," Ernesto stressed. He wondered why Lacey Serrano's parents didn't object to their daughter dating a junior. Even though Lacey and Humberto were only a year apart, it didn't seem like a good thing.

"Well, whatever. He's a jerk," Angel said. "And I think the name suits him. Anyway, Dumberto gave old Lacey a real ritzy necklace," she continued, "and she said she feels like a princess, but she's really a witch."

Richie had liked Angel from the first time he saw her, and it hurt him that Lacey and her friend, Candy, would march behind and mock Angel and her disabled grandmother. Richie knew Angel was mortified by the cruelty, and he thought many times of sneaking up behind Lacey and pulling her hair really hard, but he never did.

"I wish I was a wizard," Richie said. "I'd put a spell on Humberto and turn him into a big spider, and then I'd have him bite Lacey."

Angel giggled. "I bet she'd be scared if Dumberto turned into a spider."

"A big furry spider like a tarantula," Richie said with glee.

"Tarantulas are pretty harmless," Naomi said. "I had one as a pet when I was a little girl."

Angel stared at Naomi. "You didn't!" she cried.

"I did," Naomi laughed. "My poor mom didn't like Theodore at all, so I had to get rid of him. Theodore was my tarantula's name. I gave him to a boy I knew. The boy was really excited, and Mom was glad too."

Bobby Padilla got a serious look on his face and he said, "My mom said Humberto is an evil person."

Ernesto stiffened. He kept his voice calm. "Why does your mother think that, Bobby?"

" 'Cause everybody knows he was one of the guys who made fun of the homeless man who was murdered. They jumped around with sticks and made the man dance. Like the bull fights where they poke the bull to make him mad. My mom says

Griff Slocum mighta been a bum, but he had feelings too."

"I saw Humberto in the car with old Lacey," Richie said. "He wanted to go somewhere, and she didn't. They were sorta fighting. He slapped her in the face really hard, and her cheek was all red. I was glad he hit her. She deserved to be hit for what she did to Angel. But later on, they were laughing, so I guess she didn't mind getting slapped."

Ernesto exchanged a look with Naomi.

"Lacey likes Humberto 'cause he's rich," Bobby said.

"I don't think the Gomez family is rich," Ernesto said. "They live in an ordinary house, and Humberto drives an old car that looks like it's falling apart. The engine sounds like a threshing machine."

"I see him peeling off bills from his wallet," Bobby said.

"Yeah, he didn't used to be rich," Richie said, "but now he's got like a lot of bills and his wallet is real fat."

Ernesto glanced at Naomi again. Her eyebrows went up. They were thinking the same thing.

They all ate pieces of apple pie, finished taking pictures, and started back to the van. The freshmen took lots of good pictures of the tide pools and the volcanic rock. They seemed to have enjoyed themselves a lot. It had been a good day.

Ernesto took the freshmen home, and then he dropped off Naomi and Abel. He still had something important to do on his own, though. Ernesto did not like Lacey Serrano, but she was a fourteen-year-old girl, and she was in danger. She was hanging out with an older boy who was willing to physically abuse her. Ernesto hated that, and he felt the obligation to do something about it.

Ernesto double-checked the address of the Serrano family, and then he drove to the house on Finch Street. He had tangled with Mrs. Serrano before. He tried to get her to stop Lacey from harassing Angel Roma and her grandmother. It did not go well. Mrs. Serrano was the kind of a mother who found it very hard to think ill of her child. But still, Ernesto thought he had to try.

Ernesto rang the doorbell and waited. A nice-looking woman in a sweatshirt appeared. Ernesto recognized her immediately. "Mrs. Serrano, may I speak with you?" he asked quietly.

"Yes, of course. You're Ernesto Sandoval, aren't you? We've met before," she was cold, but polite.

"Mrs. Serrano, we've got a policy at Chavez where the seniors sort of look after the younger students, especially the freshmen. We keep an eye on the ninth graders, and when something doesn't look right, we try to alert the parents," Ernesto said.

"And what is this about exactly?" Mrs. Serrano asked in an unfriendly voice. "We are having no problems at all with our daughter. Her last report card was super. She did not make less than a B in any of her classes, and her father and I are very proud of her."

"Did you know that your daughter is dating a junior at Chavez? Somebody witnessed them in a car, and the boy slapped your daughter across the face," Ernesto said.

CHAPTER SIX

Mrs. Serrano half turned at the door and called into the house sharply. "Lacey! You come here this minute. Stop your texting and come here!"

The girl appeared, her cell phone still in hand. She glared with hatred at Ernesto Sandoval. He had gotten her in trouble before, reporting her mocking of Angel Roma and her grandmother. At first, Mrs. Serrano had defended her daughter, but then Lacey's misbehavior was proven. "What do you want?" the girl asked in a sullen voice.

"This young man claims you are dating a boy from the junior class who was seen striking you," Mrs. Serrano said in an angry voice. "You *know* you have no permission to date older boys, and if he is violent, then—"

"It's a dirty lie," Lacey snarled. "Ernesto Sandoval is a dirty liar, and he's always hated me."

"The guy's name is Humberto Gomez, and everybody at school sees them together," Ernesto said.

"Lacey," Mrs. Serrano said, "I want the truth. This young man claims you are dating the Gomez boy, and that he slapped you in the face!"

Lacey laughed sarcastically. "Oh, what a lie! I don't even know anybody in the junior class. This guy is crazy, Mom. He makes trouble for everybody. He's like a little tyrant sticking his nose into everybody's business. I swear, Mom, I don't even know who this Gomez guy is," she said.

Mrs. Serrano turned to Ernesto. "I have to trust my daughter. If she says she's not dating a boy from the junior class, then I have to believe her," she said.

Ernesto kept his voice calm and polite. "Mrs. Serrano, Humberto Gomez gave your daughter a very expensive necklace from Osterman's. He drives her around in his car, and she's with him every chance she gets. It's up to you if you want to believe me or not. I have done my duty in telling you, so I'll be going now."

Ernesto turned and walked back to his Volvo. Mrs. Serrano closed the front door, but Ernesto heard loud voices from inside the house.

"Lacey Serrano," her mother was screaming, "you told me you didn't harass that old crippled woman and her grand-daughter before, and it turned out to be a lie. And I had to suffer the humiliation of talking to the principal about the ugly misbehavior of my child! Is this another lie?"

"Mom," Lacey screamed back, "I never heard of Humberto Gomez. Sandoval is making it all up, Mom!"

Ernesto started the Volvo and drove home. He tried to focus on something good,

93

which was his Friday night date with Naomi. There was a really good mystery/ghost story out. It was in 3D, and it was getting rave reviews. Naomi didn't like regular horror movies, like the slasher flicks, but she wanted to see this one. "Chain saws just totally gross me out," Naomi said. "But this movie is supposed to send chills up your spine in a tasteful way. I'm really anxious to see it. It's fun to be scared, but not to be grossed out."

Ernesto was hugely in favor of seeing the movie too. Even when he took Naomi to slightly scary movies, she was prone to snuggle up to him. He would obligingly put his arm around her shoulders, and it was pretty cool. He hoped this movie was scary enough to give him more cuddle time in the theater.

And then, if they went somewhere to eat and bought take-out food, maybe Naomi would still be a little scared, and they could snuggle in the car.

Ernesto preferred action movies with

wild special effects. He loved the pirate movies and the superhero sagas. The more special effects, the better.

The week went by quickly. On Friday night, Ernesto drove to Naomi's house with high expectations for a romantic night. He had successfully pushed the murder of Griff Slocum from his mind, at least for now.

Ernesto always went to the door of the Martinez house and rang the bell when he was picking up Naomi. He had no use for guys who sat in their cars waiting for the chick to come out and jump in. To Ernesto, this was disrespectful to the girl and her family.

"Hey, Ernie," Felix Martinez said when he opened the door. "Come on in. Naomi is getting all painted up in there. I don't know why. You're going to the movies, and it'll be dark in there so you won't see her makeup, but still she has to slather on all the goo."

"Naomi would look beautiful if she didn't wear any makeup at all," Ernesto said.

"Yeah," Mr. Martinez said, "but try telling that to a female."

Ernesto smiled as Naomi came down the hall. Her thick dark hair was swirling gently around her oval face, and those violet eyes shone like amethysts.

"Naomi, you look awesome," Ernesto said.

"You don't look so bad yourself, babe," Naomi said. "I like you in that blue pullover."

When Ernesto and Naomi went out the door, they could still hear the conversation inside.

Linda Martinez said, "I hope they have a nice evening."

And Felix Martinez said, "Linda, I'm telling you, that Ernie is a great kid. I wish our boys had half the character he has. It makes me feel real good to think he'll probably be the one looking after our little girl."

Both Ernesto and Naomi heard her father's words, and Naomi smiled and edged closer to Ernesto, brushing a soft kiss across his cheek.

They drove to the mall and had to stand in line for twenty minutes. A lot of people had heard the buzz about the movie. During the previous night's showing, people were texting their friends that this was a "must-see." Most of the people in line were young.

After the film, which turned out to be great because Naomi clung to Ernesto the entire time, they headed for a little Mexican restaurant that served excellent shrimp tacos. They made the best shrimp tacos Ernesto ever tasted, and they were open late.

As they pulled out onto the street, a black Jeep Wrangler was behind them, right on their bumper. "Hey, dude, stop tailgating me," Ernesto said in an annoyed voice. "I'll be out of your way in a minute."

Naomi turned and looked back. "There was a black Jeep like that on our street yesterday. He kept driving up and down like he was looking for an address." The horror movie had made Naomi a little paranoid.

They turned into the parking lot of the taco place, and the Jeep continued on.

"Good riddance," Ernesto said. Then he remembered seeing a black Jeep Wrangler on *his* street yesterday too. Ernesto shrugged, and they headed into the restaurant.

Naomi and Ernesto ordered shrimp tacos and coffee, because it was a little chilly. There was a dusting of snow on the mountains in the east.

They found a secluded booth, and Naomi sat so close to Ernesto that her soft body was against his. Ernesto felt so happy. He remembered when he first laid eyes on Naomi Martinez only a little over a year ago. He and his family had just arrived from Los Angeles, and except for Abel Ruiz, Ernesto didn't have a friend at Cesar Chavez High School. Abel befriended Ernesto right away and rescued him from feeling like a completely lost soul.

Ernesto remembered looking at this beautiful girl in a pink pullover sweater and jeans that fit her like a glove. Ernesto got goose bumps just looking at her. He couldn't get the girl off his mind. That night, he dreamed about her. And then he found out she was a football player's girl-friend. Clay Aguirre and Naomi seemed very much in love. Ernesto thought sadly, "It figures."

Ernesto didn't think he had a chance with the girl, but he still dreamed about her and looked at her in class. And little by little, as Clay treated her more rudely and eventually hit her, Naomi broke from him. Ernesto moved in fast. Now, in what seemed almost like a miracle, Naomi was Ernesto's girlfriend, and he felt like the luckiest guy in the world.

When they finished eating and pulled out of the parking lot, Ernesto headed for the nearby on-ramp to the freeway. He didn't see the Jeep Wrangler that had been parked across from the taco place pull out too.

They were on the freeway when Naomi cried out, "Ernie, he's behind us! The Jeep—he's so close!"

Ernesto turned numb. He increased his speed, but the Jeep ramped up his speed too, menacing the Volvo.

Naomi looked back to see if she knew the driver, and she gasped in a trembling voice, "He's wearing a Halloween mask! Oh, Ernie. He's gonna hit us!" She grabbed her cell phone and called 911.

"There's a Jeep Wrangler behind us. He's driving real aggressively, like he wants to terrorize us … like road rage," Naomi cried into the phone, giving the location of the cars. They were coming up on the off-ramp to the *barrio*.

Suddenly, the Jeep Wrangler cut out from behind them and began to pass, but when he was even with Ernesto's Volvo, he seemed to veer into their lane, forcing Ernesto to cut sharply right. Naomi screamed, thinking the Jeep would smash into them sending the Volvo into a spin, maybe overturning it.

But Ernesto's evasive action had worked, and the Jeep sped on. Naomi leaned against Ernesto's shoulder, crying, "Oh my God, oh my God."

"He didn't have plates on the car," Ernesto said.

A police cruiser came up behind them, and Ernesto pulled off to the shoulder of the road. He gave the highway patrolman all the details, as much as he knew, and the officer took off in the direction the Jeep Wrangler had gone. Ernesto doubted they'd catch him. He was going more than a hundred miles an hour.

Ernesto was still shaking as he started the Volvo and headed for Bluebird Street.

"Ernie," Naomi asked in a wavy voice, "do you think he was just crazy? Or …"

Ernesto looked grim. "You saw a black Jeep on your street, and when you mentioned that, I remembered I saw one on Wren too. He was going slowly up and down the street. I think somebody targeted us—not us, *me*. I've made somebody real mad."

As Ernesto drove to the next street and home, he thought about what had happened, and he was sure it had something to do with the murder of Griff Slocum. He was sure of something else too. There was a deadly connection between the murder and at least one of those three guys who hassled Griff. Ernesto was digging into the crime and Rod Garcia knew it. He probably talked that over with Humberto and Rick. Whoever was driving that Jeep Wrangler, whoever was hiding behind that ugly mask was sending Ernesto a message. To keep out of this and stop trying to connect the dots.

At school on Monday, Ernesto told Abel Ruiz what had happened on the freeway. Abel's eyes narrowed. "You're dealing with bad people, homie. Let it alone. Let the cops do their job. They'll catch the rat or rats. Don't you mess with it," he said.

"You're right, Abel. I feel so guilty that Naomi was put at risk too. Whoever robbed and killed that poor homeless man was probably driving that Jeep. I don't scare easily, Abel, but I'm scared now," Ernesto confessed.

As the two boys talked, Rick Alanzar arrived on campus. Alanzar was a moody loner. He didn't seem to have any friends except for Humberto. He was usually walking alone, his hands stuck in his pockets, but today he seemed even more down than usual. He normally had bad posture, but now he was so slumped over that he looked deformed.

Alanzar met up with Humberto and they talked. They were too far away to overhear anything that was said, but Humberto seemed to get some cash from Alanzar. Both boys then walked off campus, though school was scheduled to begin in ten minutes. Neither boy came back to Chavez that day.

After school, Penelope Ruiz caught up to Ernesto on her way to Abel's car. Penelope seemed in rare high spirits. "Ernie, something awesome happened today! I can't wait to tell Abel. Old Lacey Serrano is in big trouble! You know that necklace she got from Dumberto? Well, she hid it at home, but her mother found it and, oh, wow, is she ever in trouble. Her mother grounded her, and she has to come back and forth to school in her mom's car. She can't hang with Dumberto anymore!"

Abel was walking toward his car to take Penelope home. He saw Penelope talking to Ernesto, and he hurried his pace. It looked like something big was going on.

Penelope repeated the news to her brother and said, "Oh, Mrs. Serrano just freaked. I heard Lacey whining and crying to her stupid friend, Candy Tellez, and it just opened a big hornet's nest. Old Lacey said she texted Dumberto and said it was all your fault, Ernie, 'cause you tipped off her mother about the necklace!"

CHAPTER SEVEN

Ernesto and Abel looked at each other as Penelope continued to talk. "Mrs. Serrano marched Lacey right over to the Gomez house, where Mrs. Serrano forced Lacey to give him back the necklace. Dumberto's mother was just shocked that her son had given such an expensive gift to a fourteen-year-old. She kept saying to Dumberto, 'Where did you get the money? Tell me! Did you steal the money?'"

Penelope giggled and said, "Old Lacey's life is just totally ruined now, and it couldn't happen to a better victim. She deserves it so much. She was riding high, and now she's in the pits."

Then the expression on Penelope's face

changed to one of pure happiness. "And something else awesome happened too. It's like the good fairy of happiness is smiling on me and sticking pins in Lacey. I've got a boyfriend. At last, I've got a boyfriend!"

Abel clutched his head. "Oh, give me a break!" he groaned.

"Abel, he's absolutely wonderful," Penelope cried. "His name is Gil Patone, and he's like a genius, and he's so nice and polite. You know what's best of all? He told me I was the healthiest-looking girl in the whole freshman class and that I just radiate freshness, and I wasn't all bony and sick-looking like some of the girls."

"Please tell me he's a freshman," Abel said, still clutching his head.

"He is," Penelope said. "He's just like one month older than me, and he's nice and tall, not short like most of the freshmen boys. He's sorta like you, Ernie, nice and friendly and smart, and *he really likes me!* He heard me say the other day that I like avocados, and he brought an avocado for lunch and shared it with me. He brought three avocados, in fact, and he shared with Angel and Bobby and Richie, our whole little gang. He likes us all. Is that cool or what? I mean, how many boys would be so thoughtful to do that? He's like you, Ernie. You'd do something like that."

"That's great, Penny," Ernesto said. "I'm happy for you."

"Oh, it's just about the happiest day in my whole life," Penelope said, jumping into her brother's car. "It's like I've got an amazing boyfriend, and my absolute worst enemy in the whole world, Lacey Serrano, is in the pits where she belongs. Yay."

Abel turned to Ernesto. "Stop grinning, homie. In a couple years, Kat is gonna be like this, and it'll be even worse for you 'cause Juanita is coming right up behind her. It'll be a double dose of trouble."

At the dinner table that night, Ernesto mentioned Rick Alanzar missing his English class with Ms. Lauer. Rick was not a great student, but it was his favorite class. One day, he told Ms. Lauer he wanted to write fiction like F. Scott Fitzgerald. "Rick's only friend at school is Humberto Gomez," Ernesto said.

"I went to school with two guys named Gomez," Luis Sandoval said. "The older one was Tony and the younger one was Rob. They weren't in my group of friends, but they were both terrific baseball players, Rob especially. One time, we were playing Grant, and he got three home runs. He talked about trying out for the majors. I don't know what ever happened."

"Was he a nice guy, Dad?" Ernesto asked his father.

A strange look came over Luis Sandoval's face. He just shrugged his shoulders. He didn't like to judge people. But he said, "I think Tony is Humberto's father. I've seen him at some of the parent-teacher functions. I asked him about Rob, and he said his brother had moved north."

The next day at Chavez High, Ernesto

noticed that the close friendship between Clay Aguirre and Rod Garcia at Chavez High was broken. After the bitter argument they had in the parking lot at the Our Lady of Guadalupe fiesta, the two boys ignored each other on campus. Ernesto saw them passing within three feet of one another and not saying a word.

At lunch, Naomi told Ernesto and their other friends, "Mira Nuñez said Clay is really angry at Rod over what happened to Griff Slocum. The four guys—Clay, Rod, Rick, and Humberto—had been drinking at Humberto's birthday party, and Clay got scared, so Rod pulled over. Clay said they needed to sober up. He fell asleep in Rod's Toyota, and he thought the other three had gone to get coffee like they said they were going to, but they started taunting Griff instead. Clay thinks all of it reflects badly on him, and he almost hates Rod. Mira said Clay is suspicious that maybe Rod and the others know something about who killed Griff, and that they're afraid to talk."

"I see Clay's point," Ernesto said. "He got splashed with some of the dirt 'cause he was there with them, not harassing Griff, but on the scene."

"And then for Rod to have dropped his student ID card there," Naomi said. "Mira said Clay just couldn't believe such stupidity. That's what connected the boys to the whole thing. Mira says Clay is so bitter he might never speak to Rod again. Mira is happy about that. She thinks Rod is a bad influence on Clay."

Ernesto lay back on the grass and watched the clouds floating by. When he was a small boy, he and his grandfather, his father's father, would climb a small hill near Montebello and both of them would lie on the grass like this and try to find shapes in the clouds.

Ernesto loved his grandfather. He was such a kind and gentle man. They spent many hours together, hiking, playing ball, just talking. Ernesto was a young boy when his grandfather died of a heart attack. It was the first time Ernesto had experienced deep grief. For days and even weeks, he didn't know how to cope. The most vivid memory of his grandfather's death was seeing his own father, Luis Sandoval, bent over and sobbing like a child. Up until that moment, Ernesto always saw his father as strong and unflinching in the face of anything. But when Ernesto saw his father weeping so relentlessly, it was terrifying, but also consoling in another, deeper way. It was as if Ernesto had received permission to show his own grief and to not lock it in himself. After Ernesto and his father wept together, they both began to heal.

"What are you thinking about, Ernie?" Naomi asked. She reached over and ran her fingers through Ernesto's dark hair.

"My *abuelo,* my dad's father. He died when I was a young kid. He was a great guy," Ernesto said.

"I never knew my dad's parents," Naomi said. "They were very old when I was born. My father tells me his dad was

111

pretty tough. I believe it too. I think Dad got a lot of his ways."

"I don't know if I'd ever want kids," Abel said. "It's a big hassle. I think I'd make a lousy father too. Penelope drives me crazy, and she's only my sister."

Naomi smiled. "She drives you crazy because you love her, Abel. See, those are the stirrings of a good father. You care about your little sister. A lot of boys don't care about their siblings at all," Naomi said. "How's Bianca doing?" Abel had been dating Bianca but she became dangerously thin and was diagnosed with anorexia. She had to be hospitalized.

"She's doing much better. She's gained eight pounds. Now she weighs ninety-six pounds. That doesn't sound like much, but it's a big improvement. She's eating regular food now, not just lettuce. She'll be back to Chavez in about a week. I've been seeing her in rehab. Bianca was happy to see me 'cause her mom is so busy she hardly comes around."

"See, Abel? You are a good, caring guy," Naomi said. "Perfect daddy material."

When Rick Alanzar didn't show up for school the second day, Ms. Sanchez called the Alanzar home. Rick's mother said he had the flu, but the principal was skeptical. Other students had seen him at a deli buying a lot of lottery tickets. Somebody said he spent a hundred dollars on tickets for the big weekend drawing.

Ms. Sanchez called Ernesto into her office at the end of the day. "Ernie, I know you have those great senior-to-senior programs going to help seniors in trouble, but we have a junior who seems to be slipping off track, and I wonder if you and the junior class president could pay a visit to his home. You know Angie Robledo, don't you?"

"Yeah, I work with her on junior-senior projects," Ernesto said. "She's cool."

"Well, the junior I'm worried about is Rick Alanzar. He's been a good student,

113

keeping up his GPA. His attendance record has been perfect. Now suddenly, he doesn't come to school anymore. The Alanzars live over on Polk Street, and I thought you and Angie could visit them," Ms. Sanchez said.

Ernesto was not too crazy about getting involved with Rick Alanzar after Rod Garcia's threats and what happened on the freeway the other night. He'd just about decided to stop involving himself in the situation. It seemed too dangerous. Still, he hated to turn Ms. Sanchez down, but maybe it wouldn't appear threatening to Rick if he and the junior class president went together.

"Okay, Ms. Sanchez, I'll see what I can do. My friend Abel could come with us. Abel has a good effect on those situations," Ernesto said.

"Fine," Ms. Sanchez said. "Thank you, Ernie."

Ernesto drove his Volvo over to the Alanzar house with Angie and Abel. Most of the students at Chavez High knew about Rick and the other boys harassing Griff

Slocum and getting in trouble. Due to the ages of the boys, their names weren't in the paper, but word got around.

"I don't know Rick too well," Angie said. "He's kind of a loner."

"Yeah," Ernesto said.

The Alanzar house on Polk Street was in a poorer end of town. The houses were not nearly as well kept up as the houses on the bird streets. The Alanzar house was a frame building with peeling paint, and the only greenery came from the scrawny Washington palms out front.

The three teenagers walked to the door, and a harried-looking woman answered. She self-consciously brushed back her hair with her hand. It was in disarray around her face.

Ernesto was grateful for Angie Robledo taking the initiative. "Hi, I'm the junior class president at Chavez High, Angie Robledo, and these are two students from the school, Ernesto and Abel. We're worried about Rick 'cause he's been missing school."

"He's not feeling well," Mrs. Alanzar said.

"Well," Angie said, "I've brought over a folder with the assignments he's been missing, so he can keep up. It's so easy to fall behind." She handed the folder to the woman.

"Is your husband at home?" Ernesto asked.

"No, he's a cross-country trucker. He won't be back for a week. Uh, would you like to come in? It was very nice of you to bring the makeup work," the woman said.

They entered a cramped and disorderly living room and sat down on folding chairs. Mrs. Alanzar brought three cans of cola for the students. "I hope you kids like soda," she said nervously. "Rick does. He just inhales it!"

"Has your son been to a doctor, Mrs. Alanzar?" Abel asked. "Maybe he needs antibiotics or something."

"Uh, no, it's not that. I mean, we thought he had a touch of flu, but ..." She

116

was wringing her hands. "It's more … *emotional*. Uh … you kids probably know about the bad thing that happened. I was so ashamed. That is so unlike Rick. He would never have done such a thing if he hadn't gone to that boy's birthday party and started drinking."

"Yeah," Abel said, "a lot of the kids at Chavez drink, and it causes a lot of problems."

Ernesto was again grateful for Abel being there. He was able to make Rick's action seem more normal, just the result of liquor. It put the woman at ease that these students did not see her son as a monster who had tormented a homeless man who subsequently died mysteriously.

"It was the Gomez boy's idea to do that to Mr. Slocum. Rick is a loner. He doesn't have many friends. Whatever Humberto suggests, he goes along … but, of course, the boys had nothing to do with what happened to the man later. But ever since then, Rick has not been the same. I think he

117

feels guilty about it. He didn't hurt the man. None of the boys hurt the man, and yet Rick is just so troubled by everything that happened. He's a good boy, and usually I can get through to him, but now ..." Mrs. Alanzar shook her head.

"Mrs. Alanzar," Ernesto said, "we have counselors at Chavez. Don't you think it would be good if Rick talked to one of them? It might help with the stuff that's bothering him."

"We're not rich people," Mrs. Alanzar said. "We have no money for doctors."

"No, no," Ernesto said. "The counseling is free. Rick could just make an appointment, and they'd help him through this." It crossed Ernesto's mind that kids had seen Rick spending a hundred dollars on lottery tickets in the last few days. But he didn't bring that up. There was no point.

"Well, when Rick gets home, I'll tell him about it," Mrs. Alanzar said. "Thanks so much for your concern and for bringing his makeup work."

Ernesto thought then that mentioning that his friends at Cesar Chavez High School had survived many difficulties and were now happy, successful students might encourage Mrs. Alanzar.

"There've been a lot of guys at Chavez who were in trouble with the law, Mrs. Alanzar, and now they're doing great. A couple dudes were doing graffiti all over town, and they dropped out of school in their junior year. They turned their lives around with a little help, and they're over the moon now. So Rick made a mistake that night, but it's not the end of the world," Ernesto said.

"Yeah," Angie Robledo said. "The junior year is kind of tough for a lot of kids. I have a friend who was doing great as a freshman and sophomore, then she met some friends who liked to party, and she got in a bad auto accident. She was driving drunk. Luckily, nobody was killed, but the incident almost knocked her out of the game, but now she's fine."

A distressed look came to Mrs. Alanzar's face. "I think that one of Rick's problems is his friendship with the Gomez boy. He's not a good influence on Rick. I don't like the Gomez family, to tell you the truth. Humberto has a cousin, Rod Garcia, and he's not a nice kid at all. I just hope Rick can find better friends when this is all over."

"Well," Ernesto said, getting up, "thanks for talking to us, Mrs. Alanzar, and be sure to tell Rick the counselors are great if he wants to talk to one. They're more than happy to help. And Ms. Lauer, Rick's English teacher, she sends her best wishes. She misses Rick in class. He told her he wanted to be a writer someday, and she wants to encourage him."

Mrs. Alanzar's expression softened a bit. "Yes, Rick talks about Ms. Lauer all the time. He really enjoys that class. I think she's been his favorite teacher," she said. "Thanks so much for coming by. It's really nice that you guys care about each student like this. I'm sure it will mean a lot to Rick that you took the time and trouble to bring the makeup work and express your concern."

"Tell Rick to come back to school as quick as he can," Angie said. "We're going to start reading F. Scott Fitzgerald's *The Great Gatsby*. He likes Fitzgerald so that's gonna be fun."

"Thank you so much," the woman said. Her voice was a little shaky. She seemed like a nice person, and Ernesto felt sorry for her. Clearly there were problems, but it was not their business to go any deeper. They had done what Ms. Sanchez asked, and now the three of them went to the door and left.

Angie Robledo took a deep breath as they walked to the car. "Did you guys get the same vibes I got? You can just feel the tension in that house. It hangs like a heavy wet curtain."

"She seems like a nice lady," Abel said. "Probably a good mom. I'm thinking that something's wrong, though, and she knows something's wrong, but she's not sure

121

what. Rick maybe knows more about what happened to Griff Slocum than he's saying, and that's what's making him sick. He's trapped in a box of silence, and he doesn't know where the key is."

"Yeah," Ernesto said. "I'm getting that too. Maybe Humberto or Rick or even Rod Garcia noticed how Griff was grasping that leather pouch on the chain around his neck. He wouldn't let go of it, so they knew there had to be something in there. And there was. The police said he had something of value that was taken. So one of them went back later and tried to get the thing, whatever it was, and Griff fought for it. He fought to the death for it." Ernesto was strident.

"And the other two guys sort of know what went down, and the guy who got the thing … he's paying them off to keep quiet. That's why Humberto and Rick all of a sudden have money. I can't figure who might have done it. If Rick's feeling guilty, then it must not be him. If it was Rod or Humberto, Rick doesn't want to tell on them."

Angie Robledo's eyes were wide with shock. "Are you guys saying that you think one of those three murdered somebody?" she asked.

Ernesto shrugged. "Or knows who did," he said.

"What's the way out of a thing like that?" Abel asked, a bewildered look on his face.

"The truth," Ernesto said. "The truth, man. Rick Alanzar is seventeen years old. He can't keep this bottled inside himself for the rest of his life. If Gomez or Garcia did it, they gotta pay for it."

"What if Rick did it?" Abel asked.

"Then he's got to pay, but I don't think he did," Ernesto said. "Gomez is a bully. He's violent. He's already got a little fourteen-year-old girlfriend he's slapping around."

"You know, man," Abel said, "when a dude is juiced on booze or drugs, he's not the same person. Maybe Rick is a quiet little loner when he's sober, but maybe the

123

liquor brought out a whole different person. The family is poor. Maybe the guy looks around the broken-down house and figures he's going nowhere, just like his father, you know? And suddenly he sees the homeless guy clutching at the leather pouch, and he's so drunk he doesn't care about anything but getting whatever is in there. What the poor bum is willing to die for."

"So what are you guys going to do?" Angie asked.

Ernesto remembered that night on the freeway. He remembered the terror on Naomi's face. His jaw tightened. "Nothing," he said. "There's nothing I can do."

CHAPTER EIGHT

On Saturday morning, Abel Ruiz got a frantic phone call from the younger student he was paired with in the student mentoring program, Bobby Padilla. The boy had been living with his mother since she had separated from his father, who used to whip Bobby when he misbehaved. Now Bobby was out of his mind with fear.

"Abel, you gotta help me," he cried. "My father is coming tomorrow to visit. I'm so scared. He's gonna ask me about school and stuff, and I got a C-minus in math. He's gonna criticize everything about me. Pretty soon he's gonna get mad and take off his belt and wallop me, Abel, like he used to do. I don't wanna see him, Abel."

"But he's probably coming down to see *you,* dude," Abel said. "He and your mom are quits, so he's not coming to see her."

"But I don't wanna see him," Bobby wailed. "You gotta come get me, Abel, until he's gone."

Only a few months ago, when Bobby thought his mother was going to send him to live with his father, the boy ran away and hid out in an abandoned warehouse for a week.

"Okay, homie, listen," Abel said. "I'll help you out, but I gotta figure out what to do. Put your mom on."

After a few seconds, Mrs. Padilla was on the phone. "Abel," she said, sounding almost as upset as her son, "I don't know what to do. My ex-husband has the right to see his son. The court order says so. He's never been arrested for abuse or anything, and he swears to me he doesn't drink anymore. He's even taken anger management classes. It will only be for Sunday, and then he goes away."

"Mrs. Padilla," Abel said, "how does this sound? I'll come over for Sunday dinner too. I'll cook it. I'll make one of my good dinners. I'll hang around until your ex-husband is gone. That way, Bobby will feel safe, and the father can visit with his kid."

"Oh, Abel," Mrs. Padilla said, "would you do that? Oh, that would be so wonderful. Thank you." She told Bobby, then handed the phone to him.

"Abel, you'll come for sure? You promise?" Bobby asked. "You'll be here the whole time?"

"Yeah, dude. Your mom said your father is coming at twelve, and I'll be there at eleven thirty to get lunch going. I'll hang out with you guys until your father leaves. You got nothing to worry about, okay?" Abel said. "And who knows? This might be a good thing. You remember your father at his worst, but maybe he's been missing you and feels bad for the mean things he did. This could be the start of something good."

"How come you're gonna cook the meal?" Bobby asked.

"I told you guys," Abel laughed. "I'm studying to be a chef. I'm gonna practice on your family."

"We eat mostly out of cans and stuff. We eat spaghetti and meatballs and macaroni and cheese. My mom cleans houses, and she's too tired to make other stuff. But that's okay. I like mac and cheese. And pork and beans. You gonna bring some cans, Abel?" Bobby asked.

"No, I cook from scratch," Abel said.

"What's that mean?" Bobby asked.

"It means I don't use cans, Bobby," Abel said.

"Wow," Bobby said. "You must be like a magician. You're sure you're coming, huh?"

"Yeah, I'm sure. See you around eleven thirty, dude," Abel said.

When Abel ended the call, his mother rushed at him, her face wreathed in joy. "Oh, Abel, exciting news! Your brother, Tomás, just called, and he's been accepted to the top honor society in the nation. It looks like he's going to be Phi Beta Kappa!"

"That's great, Mom," Abel said. Tomás, the eldest Ruiz, was smart, handsome, and charming, and now Phi Beta Kappa?

"Who were you on the phone with, Abel?"

"Oh, Bobby Padilla, the freshman I mentor. I'm gonna go over there and make dinner for him, his mom, and her ex. The kid is afraid of the ex, so I'm gonna hang around to make him feel better," Abel said.

Liza Ruiz began to smile dreamily, "You know, Tomás is so adorable. Such a great honor, and he isn't bragging or anything. He just sort of dropped the news like it wasn't important."

Liza Ruiz looked ecstatic over her older son's newest triumph.

Penelope looked up from her computer. "You know what, Mom?" she said coldly. "Abel is giving up his whole Sunday when he was looking forward to hanging with his friends. He's giving it up to help a kid he isn't even related to. I think that's awesome, Mom."

Now Mrs. Ruiz looked embarrassed. "Oh, of course it is. You're such a good person, Abel. I'm so proud of how compassionate you are. That little boy—Roddy—he is so lucky to have you as a friend."

"His name is Bobby, Mom," Penelope growled. "Bobby Padilla. Abel has told us that a dozen times."

Abel cast his sister a quick smile. Mom wasn't trying to be thoughtless. She really did love Abel and Penelope as much as she loved Tomás, her perfect child. It was just that she was so thrilled by the level of his success that sometimes it blinded her to everything and *everybody* else.

Abel went to the supermarket to pick up what he needed for tomorrow's dinner at the Padilla's. Like many in the *barrio*, they were poor and didn't eat fresh food. On her way home from her backbreaking housecleaning jobs, Mrs. Padilla picked up cheap cans from the thrift store, buying whatever was on sale. Abel wanted to make tomorrow special, so he bought two pounds of sirloin steak, leeks, frozen broccoli, carrots, water chestnuts, and red peppers. He had chili puree and garlic at home. The prep time would be short, and it wouldn't take long to cook. Abel cut the sirloin into small strips so he'd be ready to go. Since he started working at the Sting Ray, he was making good money on tips. It fascinated some of the regular customers to see the young chef come to their table, and they were very generous.

When Abel pulled his car into the Padilla driveway on Sunday, Bobby was at the door. "You came!" he shouted.

"Of course I came," Abel laughed. "You think I'm a liar, homie?"

"You're all right, Abel," Bobby cried, turning toward the inside of the house. "Mom! Abel came!"

Mrs. Padilla appeared in a faded print dress. She was a very pretty woman, but hard work and worry had taken their toll. She looked older than her years. "This is so nice of you, Abel," she said. "A young man your age, I bet you had other plans for today, and you canceled them to do this."

"No, no," Abel lied. Actually he was going to meet Ernesto, Paul, and Julio to watch auto racing.

Abel went into the small kitchen and went to work. The stove didn't work too well, but Abel brought his cookware from home and cooked the beef and leeks efficiently. He had put the lemon meringue pie he made the night before in the refrigerator.

At quarter to twelve, the doorbell rang.

"Ohhh," Bobby groaned.

"Don't sweat it, dude," Abel said with a wink. "We can do this."

A burly man dressed in jeans and a checkered shirt came into the living room. Bobby was on the frail side. He took after his mother who probably didn't weight much more than a hundred ten pounds. The man was well muscled and formidable.

Abel could understand the boy's consternation when this dude got angry.

"Hello, Mel," Mrs. Padilla said.

"Hello, Clare," he said uneasily.

Abel decided to make things easier by introducing himself. "I'm Abel Ruiz, a senior at Cesar Chavez High School. I'm studying to be a chef, and I'm a friend of Bobby's. I'm cooking dinner today to get some practice." Abel extended his hand. "You must be Bobby's father. Nice to meet you."

"Nice to meet you too," the man said.

Bobby finally found the courage to emerge from the kitchen. He stood beside Abel and said in a squeaky voice, "Hi, Dad."

"Hello, Bobby," Mr. Padilla said. "You've grown so much since ... I hardly recognize you."

"My," Mrs. Padilla said, "something smells good from the kitchen."

They gathered around the table and Abel served sirloin in spicy chili sauce over rice. Bobby's eyes got really big when he tasted the steak. "It's so tender. I never tasted meat like this before. It's so good," he said.

"Bobby is doing really well in school," Mrs. Padilla told her ex-husband. "He's raised his math grade from a D to a C, and he used to be getting Cs in English but now he got a B-plus. His grade point average is a B now."

"That's very good to hear," Mr. Padilla said. He looked at his son and smiled. "Good for you."

Abel had told Bobby to talk about sports, so after a moment, he said, "I'm going out for basketball at school."

"You've gotten so much taller," Mr. Padilla said. "You'll be good at basketball."

"Yeah, me and my friend Richie, we're both gonna be on the Cougar team," Bobby said. He didn't seem as scared of his father as when the man first appeared.

"You'll need good basketball shoes," Mr. Padilla said.

"Oh, Richie got a nice pair for his birthday from his friend Ernie," Bobby said.

"I'll take care of that for you, Bobby," the man said.

As they finished the meal, Bobby said, "I think this is the best meal I ever had in my whole life!"

Abel brought out the lemon pie, and though it didn't seem possible that Bobby's eyes could grow any larger, they did.

After dinner, Abel noticed the man looking at his son and trying to decide if he could take the next step. It seemed he was as nervous about being with Bobby as Bobby was being with him, maybe more so. Finally the man said, "I saw a hoop out on the garage, Bobby. Want to shoot some baskets?"

"Uh …" Bobby looked at Abel. Abel smiled and gave a thumbs-up. "Yeah, I guess so," Bobby said. Bobby was still not comfortable with his father, but he was trying to do the right thing. Abel was proud of him for that.

The father and son went out to shoot some baskets, and Abel joined them as a spectator. "I'm so bad at basketball that they begged me not to join the team," Abel explained as he sat in a lawn chair to watch.

After about ten minutes, the man and boy seemed to be getting along, so Abel went back in the house to give them some privacy.

"Bobby," Mr. Padilla said when he was alone with his son. "I've been a lousy father."

Bobby just looked at his father in silence. He didn't know what to say. The man continued, "I didn't mean to be so hard on you. I just did it the way my father did. He beat us all, my brothers and me. When you started skipping school and getting in trouble, I thought we were losing you. I thought you needed discipline, and I didn't know anything but the belt."

Bobby's mouth was very dry. He'd never seen his father like this before. He always seemed tough and strong and mean, but now he was humble. Bobby couldn't think of anything to say.

Mr. Padilla said, "I've got a better job now. I'm going to be sending you and your mom more support money. She won't have to work so hard. Things will be better, Bobby. I swear it."

"That'd be good," Bobby finally said. "Mom's real tired all the time. She works real hard."

"I know. Your mom is a good woman. I never deserved her," Mr. Padilla said. "I don't expect her ever to forgive me, and I don't expect you to either. I was mean to both of you. I drank up most of what I made. I hung out at night with my friends like I wasn't even married. So I'm not asking for forgiveness. It's too late for that. I just want a little bit of a relationship with you, Bobby, because you're my son, and I love you."

Bobby made a basket and his father said, "You're good. You got the right moves. I'll be bringing down the new shoes next weekend."

"Thanks," Bobby said.

Mr. Padilla thanked his ex-wife for having him, and he thanked Bobby for being polite. He thanked Abel for the wonderful meal. Then, at two o'clock, he walked down the driveway to his pickup truck. He was getting in the truck when Bobby said, "Dad?"

"Yeah, Bobby," the man said, turning.

"I forgive you," Bobby said. His voice broke then and he said, "I'm, uh, … glad you came. It's okay if you come back some more."

"Bobby," Mr. Padilla said, "you just made my day. You've made my world."

Mr. Padilla drove away, heading north.

The Gomez family lived in a green stucco house at the far end of Sparrow Street where Abel lived. As Abel turned into his driveway, he saw a lot of police action at the Gomez house. Abel called Ernesto.

"How'd the dinner at the Padilla's go, homie?" Ernesto asked.

"Great, man. Lot of healing took place. But, Ernie, you know Humberto Gomez lives at the end of my street, and right now the cops are swarming all over the place," Abel said.

"No kidding, man. Can you see what's happening?" Ernesto asked.

"No, but after I park, I'm taking a walk down there. Lot of people standing around. Maybe somebody knows something. I'll keep you posted," Abel said.

Abel got fairly close to the Gomez house just as two officers came out with Humberto Gomez. He wasn't handcuffed, but his parents looked distraught. It looked like he was going down to the police station voluntarily to answer some questions. Humberto had already given the police a statement about what had happened that night, but they apparently wanted more information.

Humberto got into the police cruiser and they drove off, followed by a second police car. The parents stepped back in the house, probably to call a lawyer.

"Ernie," Abel said into his cell phone, "Humberto Gomez left with the cops. He wasn't being arrested. I guess they just want to talk to him some more. I'm pretty sure that those dudes hassling Griff Slocum and his death are connected. I can't figure how, but it wasn't a coincidence."

When Abel got back to his house, his mother was on the phone. "What did they say exactly?" she was asking. "Oh, well, I'm sure they just need him as a witness or something … I know. … I know, Juanita. Kids will get themselves into bad situations because they're just not thinking straight … Well, Juanita, I *know* that. I've known Berto since he was a little boy, and he's a bit wild, but most boys are. Even my Tomás, who's about as perfect as a boy can be, drank too much one night when he was a junior in high school and drove his car right up on the lawn of the neighbor's house. He took out all their oleanders." Liza Ruiz shook her head. "We were mortified. Well, Juanita, you just keep the faith. It'll be all right."

When Abel's mother put down the phone, she turned to Abel. "That was poor Juanita Gomez, Humberto's mother. She's all upset. The police came to the door and asked if Humberto could come downtown and give them more information about the night that poor homeless man died. I'm sure it's nothing, but Juanita is so upset. It's so unfortunate that those three boys were playing tricks on the homeless man just before someone else came along and killed him. It's such a dreadful coincidence. I'm sure those boys meant no real harm, but it just looks suspicious," she said.

"It looks more than suspicious," Abel said. "Three guys harassing Mr. Slocum and then, about an hour later, we're supposed to believe some other dude comes along and murders the poor guy. There's a connection, Mom. Something that happened when those guys were tormenting Mr. Slocum led to him getting killed."

"Oh, Abel, I'm sure you're wrong. It's just absolutely inconceivable that those boys from Chavez would have had anything to do with that terrible crime," Mrs. Ruiz said. "It had to be a stranger. Some monster lurking in the shadows who happened to come along and murder the poor man, maybe over a cigarette or something. Those people who live on the street, they fight and die over meaningless things. That's the way they are."

Abel was waiting for his mother to ask him how things went at the Padilla house. Was Bobby Padilla okay with the father he feared? Did the meal go well? Did the Padillas like that expensive steak Abel bought?

But instead, Abel's mother said, "I sympathize so much with poor Juanita Gomez. Abel, do you remember when you got into that terrible mess with the daughter of the donut lady? The girl ran away from home, and when the police came banging on our door, I almost died! I was so frightened. I thought they were going to arrest you, Abel, and take you away. I was crying and shaking. I can understand what poor

Juanita Gomez is going through. Only a mother knows what another mother feels like when her child is under suspicion!"

"Mom," Abel said bitterly, "I didn't do anything wrong, remember? The lady in the donut shop, Elena, she let her little girl roam the streets at all hours. Mrs. Sandoval took the girl home that night, but she got out again because the mother was too drunk to watch her kid. The police didn't accuse me of anything because I didn't do anything. You were acting crazy, but there was no excuse for that. This thing with Humberto Gomez is different. He and his friends taunted and mocked a poor homeless guy, and it somehow probably led to his death. That's way different, Mom."

"Well," Liza Ruiz said in a hurt voice, "I wasn't implying—"

Abel walked down the hall and slammed the door.

CHAPTER NINE

Humberto Gomez had never been so scared in all his life. He sat at the police officer's desk, the palms of his hands sweating. He wiped them on his trousers. His parents had wanted to come with him, and the police said they could, but Humberto didn't want that. He said he could handle it himself because he had done nothing wrong besides making fun of an old bum. It was mean and stupid to do that, Humberto admitted, but he was drunk, and he didn't know what he was doing. Humberto did not want his parents to have to hear the details of the ugly incident all over again because he was so embarrassed that he'd done something like that.

Sergeant Arriola, a police investigator with short, dark curly hair and a no-nonsense approach said, "Humberto, I know you told us about this before, but now, in your own words, tell me what happened that night as best you can remember."

"Well, some of my friends threw a birthday bash for me at a condo, and we got to drinking. Somebody brought cases of beer. Clay Aguirre, Rod Garcia—my cousin—and Rick Alanzar, the four of us, we finally left the party in Rod's car. We were all buzzed. Rod was driving 'cause he claimed he wasn't as drunk as the rest of us. But Clay got sick. Rod pulled over so Clay could try to sleep it off. Rod didn't wanna get nailed by the cops. We were gonna go get some coffee or something, then come back to the car."

Sergeant Arriola asked, "And what did you do?"

"Well, we were walking to the corner to this all-night store to get coffee, and we seen this homeless guy stumbling around. He was a little drunk too. We thought it'd be fun to play tricks on him. Um, we, uh, got some sticks, just wooden slats that were laying there by a store, and we pretended he was a bull and we were matadors, and we kinda surrounded him and yelled and stuff. He got all upset, jumping this way and that, and we were laughing 'cause it was funny. But we didn't hit him with the sticks. We didn't touch him. We didn't hurt the guy, I swear," Humberto said. He wiped the damp palms of his hands on his trousers again.

"And then what happened?" Sergeant Arriola asked.

"These two guys, gangbangers, you know, came along. Real mean guys. Everybody is scared of them. They tag and stuff. Dom Reynosa and Carlos Negrete. They're gangbangers," Humberto said.

"Yes, you said they were gangbangers twice," Sergeant Arriola said.

"Anyway, they grabbed these big palm fronds ... those things are sharp. They can cut you bad. They started yelling at us and swinging those sharp palm fronds, and we took off 'cause we didn't want to mess with bad dudes like them," Humberto said.

"Why do you think they did that, Humberto?" Sergeant Arriola asked.

"Uh, well … they were mad that we were, you know, kinda playing tricks on the bum. I guess they were friends of his or something. But we weren't hurting him. We were just sort of playing around." Humberto was aware of the look of disgust on the woman's face and he said, "We never touched him. We didn't bruise him or anything."

"And then what did you do, Humberto?" Sergeant Arriola asked.

"We went to Rod's car where Clay was sleeping. We woke him up. Told him what happened. He yelled and cussed at us. He got so mad he kinda sobered up. He called his girlfriend, Mira Nuñez, to come get him. She did. Then Rod, he dropped me and Rick at my house 'cause Rick didn't wanna go home drunk. We hung out there till morning. My old man wasn't there, but Uncle Rob was, and we told him what happened and he laughed. He's real cool," Humberto said.

Sergeant Arriola's eyes narrowed, and she leaned forward. "I want to ask you something now, Humberto, that is very important. I want you to think hard of the time when you and Rod and Rick were poking at Mr. Slocum and pretending he was a bull. Did you notice that the man had a chain around his neck that held a leather pouch?"

"Uh, yeah. I saw that. I saw him kinda clutching at it as we were playing with him, like he was afraid he'd lose it or something. It was funny 'cause it was just a piece of junk with maybe a few dollars in it. But he acted like it was something important," Humberto said. "I told my uncle Rob, and he said sometimes these old bums have more money than we think. Maybe that's why he was protecting the pouch, but I remember kinda seeing something half spill out, and it wasn't even money."

148

Sergeant Arriola asked, "What did the thing that half spilled out look like?"

"Nothin'," Humberto said. "A card of some kind with somebody's picture on it, like they put in cereal boxes."

"Maybe a baseball card?" Sergeant Arriola asked.

Humberto shrugged. "Maybe. I don't know," he said. "Then Uncle Rob laughed when I told him that the bum was protecting an old card from a cereal box or something."

"Humberto," Sergeant Arriola said. "You need to call your parents. They might want to get you legal representation."

Humberto Gomez paled. He had no feeling in his arms or legs. "But I didn't do nothin'," he cried.

"Humberto, we have information that you have recently been spending large sums of money on gifts for a girl at your school and on other things. Right after the death of Mr. Slocum, you seemed to be spending freely although your family is not rich," Sergeant Arriola said.

"No, see, you don't get it. Uncle Rob gave me and Rick and Rod some money. He said he made a lucky bet and stuff … just a couple hundred. My uncle Rob was the one who gave us the money," Humberto stammered.

"Why did he do that?" Sergeant Arriola asked. "So you'd keep your mouth shut about something you may have suspected or would come to suspect?"

Humberto sank deeply in the chair. "I wanna call my parents," he said.

Arturo Sandoval came down to the police station just as Rick Alanzar and his mother were arriving. Sandoval was representing both boys. Rick Alanzar was sobbing as he walked beside his mother. Her arm was around his shoulders.

When Rick sat down with Sergeant Arriola, he was shaking. "I haven't been able to get it off my mind that it's our fault the guy died," Rick cried. "We went back to the house and told that snake about the bum and his leather pouch, about the card. Rob

Gomez, he's into baseball. He figured it was a valuable card. He left the house right away. I could see it in his eyes, and then … Rod Garcia, the creep, he told his cousin's uncle that Ernesto Sandoval was stirring up trouble, trying to link the harassment of the homeless guy to his murder, and the sneak said he'd come down in his Jeep Wrangler and put the fear of the Lord into Sandoval. I don't know what he did, but Sandoval got quiet about the incident after that."

Both Humberto Gomez and Rick Alanzar were released to their families pending juvenile court hearings to determine if they had concealed important information from the police. Arturo Sandoval assured the court that both boys would return for their hearings and would accept whatever punishment they got. Meanwhile, the police in Los Angeles were closing in on Gomez. He had a long criminal record, and he was presently on parole for stealing a valuable painting from a local museum.

At the Sandoval home that night, Ernesto

said, "I'm at least glad that those kids from Chavez weren't the ones who killed Griff Slocum. Yeah, they taunted him, but they didn't harm him physically. It would have been awful if they'd been the ones who hit him with the pipe."

"Isn't it terrible that *any* human being would love money so much that they'd kill a man over a baseball card that was valuable?" Maria Sandoval said.

"It *was* a Honus Wagner card," Ernesto said. "That leaked out. It must be worth a lot, even in less-than-mint condition."

"Poor Griff," Luis Sandoval said. "That card was his only treasure. He probably fought for it with his last ounce of strength. The poor guy used to find a little joy in small things, Ernie. Remember when you bought him a sub sandwich that day? He loved the jalapeño peppers. He even laughed when they were burning his tongue."

"Yeah," Ernesto said. "I'm glad I did a few things for him. It makes me feel better, you know?"

Katalina Sandoval said, "I hope they catch that bad man who hurt Mr. Slocum and put him in jail for two hundred years."

With all the dramatic news of the solving of the Griff Slocum murder, Maria Sandoval had held back on announcing her own big news. "You guys," she said with a triumphant grin, "My *Don't Blink, It's a Skink* book is doing pretty well. I got a royalty check last week, and I was really excited. We're not rich or anything, but it'll cover six mortgage payments!"

"Congratulations, Mom," Ernesto said. "That's super. But don't spend it all on mortgage payments. Get something awesome for yourself too."

Luis Sandoval said, "Right on. Wow, Maria, before long you'll be making more money on your writing than I'm making teaching. Not that you'd have to do that well to surpass me. With all the budget cuts, we don't even mention the word 'raise' anymore in the faculty lounge."

Several days passed before the police

caught up to Gomez. He had fled his apartment and run the Jeep Wrangler over a cliff in the Santa Monica Mountains. The police found him hiding in a cheap hotel in Houston, Texas. He still had the Honus Wagner baseball card in his possession.

Griff Slocum's only living relative, his mother, was contacted and told the news. Mrs. Slocum had mixed feelings about seeing the card for the first time in twenty years. She knew her son had it those many years ago, but she was sure he had long since used it for his drug habit. She was astonished that the Honus Wagner had survived with him for so long. The card was from Griff's grandfather.

When Penelope Ruiz, Richie Loranzo, Bobby Padilla, and Angel Roma met for lunch in their usual spot, there was a newcomer—Gil Patone. Gil was a cute freshman with lots of curly hair and none of the problems that beset his new circle of friends. Gil came from a happy family consisting of four children, and although his parents were lower middle class, they were getting along fine.

Gil Patone really did like Penelope, and he was very appreciative of the times her brother Abel made tortillas for the whole gang. Today was one of those times.

"I got a new pair of athletic shoes from my dad," Bobby Padilla said. "Now I can really play good basketball."

"I thought your dad was mean," Angel Roma said.

"He was sorta, but he's better now," Bobby said.

Richie Loranzo said, "Ernie got me a cool pair of athletic shoes for my birthday."

"We'll all root for you guys when you play," Angel said. She really liked Richie Loranzo.

"I'm not much for sports," Gil admitted. "But I love science. I'm gonna be a scientist, I think."

"Do scientists make a lot of money?" Angel asked.

"I guess so," Gil said. "If they invent something really good. Like maybe an energy source for cars that's clean and renewable and stuff."

"Basketball players make a lot of money," Richie Loranzo said. "They make millions and millions."

"Yeah," Bobby said, "I wish I could be a really famous basketball player. I'd buy my mom a big house near the ocean or something, and she'd never have to clean houses again. Her back hurts all the time. Dad said he's gonna send more money so she doesn't have to work so hard. I hope he does."

"You know what?" Angel Roma said with a wistful look on her face. "I wish somebody would invent something that'd make my grandmother's Parkinson's disease go away. I remember being real little and she was sick, but it wasn't bad then. We had a lot of fun. It's hard to understand her now when she talks, and she shakes a lot. I know she feels really bad about being like that. I take my grandma for walks every day, and I don't mind it now that horrible Lacey and Candy don't march behind us making fun of us."

"I'm so glad Lacey's in trouble with her mom for going out with that creepy Dumberto Gomez and taking that expensive necklace from him," Penelope said. "I hope she stays grounded all year. She deserves it."

"It was on TV that the homeless man was killed for his baseball card," Gil said. "It was a Honus Wagner. I guess that's the best baseball card in the world 'cause he was such a good player, and it's so old and there aren't many of them around."

"I heard it might be worth hundreds of thousands or something," Richie said.

"The police found the card. The murderer still had it. The guy on TV said it belongs to the dead man's mother now because there was a paper in his pocket, like a will, saying that if he died, his treasure should go to his mother. I guess she's an old lady," Bobby said. "Maybe she'll go on an ocean cruise all around the world now and see every country."

"Maybe she'll buy a whole pile of diamonds," Angel said.

"I guess she could have just about anything she wanted," Penelope said.

"I bet the old lady will be real sad when she sees the baseball card," Angel said. "Because her son died to keep it. He must have fought real hard with the bad guy to try to keep it, but the bad guy was stronger and hit him in the head and killed him. I don't think I have anything at all that I would die for."

"Me neither," Gil Patone said. "I got some really cool skateboards and a surfboard too, but I wouldn't die for them."

"I got nothing I'd die to keep," Bobby said. "Not even my new athletic shoes."

Penelope laughed. "Well, that's pretty obvious, Bobby, 'cause if you died to save your athletic shoes, you wouldn't need them anymore, right?"

They all laughed then.

Penelope lay back on the grass and said, "I'd like to have a lot of money. I'd do some good things and some selfish things. I'd give some to my dad, 'cause he's like your mom, Bobby. He works real hard every day putting in cement walls and stuff, and his back hurts like crazy. I'd give him enough money so he didn't have to work like that anymore. And I'd help Abel with the tuition for chef school. And then I'd buy some awesome clothes for myself, just like those actresses wear when they walk on the red carpet."

Bobby Padilla said, "I'd buy a real cool car, maybe a race car so everybody would look when it went down the street."

"You're not old enough to drive, Bobby," Penelope said.

"I'd keep it in the garage and polish it every day so it'd look really good when I get to be sixteen and get my driver's license," Bobby said.

"How about you, Angel?" Penelope asked. "What would you do with lots of money?"

"I'd find some doctor who could cure

Grandma, and I'd give him the money he wanted," Angel said.

Gil Patone looked serious. "I don't think there is such a doctor, Angel. If there was, he'd probably do it even if you didn't give him lots of money."

Gil Patone finished the tortilla Abel had given them and lay back on the grass, looking up at the cloudless sky. "If I had a ton of money, I'd make sure every single kid everywhere on Earth could get educated and go to college and be somebody wonderful. That's what I'd do." He sighed.

"You know," he continued, "there are millions of kids in this world who will never even learn to read and write. Can you just imagine what the world would be like if every kid got the chance to be educated? Now all those millions of brains are being lost. We'd have an amazing world if they all got the chance. It'd change the world. There's a kid in El Salvador or the Congo or maybe even in the *barrio* right here, who could cure cancer or Parkinson's, but that kid will never get the chance," Gil said.

They were all silent then.

The bell rang for afternoon classes, and they got up slowly, brushing the grass off their jeans.

Penelope Ruiz walked with Gil to their next class, which was English. Gil had told Penelope that he liked her, that she was cool. He told her that several times, but still Penelope wondered. Did he really, *really* like her? They neared English, and Gil reached over and grasped Penelope's hand. Penelope thought she would die of happiness.

CHAPTER TEN

Julio Avila was driving to Cesar Chavez High School in his ancient pickup early the next morning. He wanted to get in some practice running before classes. A track meet was coming up, and he wanted to finish big. Every time he ran he got a little faster, and he really wanted to leave Rod Garcia in his dust.

But in the foggy early morning, Julio caught sight of his father looking for cans and bottles in a dumpster along Washington Street. He was taking out the aluminum soda cans. When he filled a bag, he was able to make several dollars. Julio felt sick. His father had a small disability pension, and he used that to pay their rent at the trailer park.

Julio bought their food and paid their utilities and other expenses from his job at the supermarket. Things were always tight. There was little or nothing left over for extras.

Julio felt so sorry that his father couldn't afford a few little pleasures, like a beer with his friends. When Mr. Avila had taken Griff Slocum out for fish and chips and beer, it was a real stretch. He'd saved for two weeks, collecting bottles and doing odd jobs.

Julio knew his father loved chocolate bars, so he bought some. But Mr. Avila frowned and said, "Son, you shouldn't be spending your hard-earned money on stuff I don't need. God knows I'm enough of a burden on you as it is."

Julio felt so bad that his father had to humiliate himself scrounging for empty cans and bottles for the recycling center. Mr. Avila had worked hard in his life, and, yeah, he'd made plenty mistakes, but who was perfect? Julio felt that most of his father's hard life was the result of bad breaks, rather than his vices. Julio thought his father was a good man, and nobody loved their son more than Mr. Avila loved Julio.

Julio entertained fantasies of coming into a lot of money and being able to give his father a little dignity in the few years he had left. He wasn't a healthy man, and if something good didn't happen soon, Julio was afraid any good fortune would come too late.

When Julio finished running that morning, he saw Ernesto Sandoval just coming to school.

"Hey, Julio," Ernesto said. "You put me to shame. Out running already. I'm sitting there wolfing down Mom's eggs, and you're burning up the course. No wonder you're so much better than me!" Then Ernesto noticed the glum look on his friend's face. "What's up, dude? Having a bad day already?"

Julio shrugged. "On my way in, I saw my dad looking for cans and bottles in the dumpsters on Washington. He's trying to get enough together to buy himself a beer or maybe a chocolate bar. It tears me apart to see him like that. I offered to give him some more money from my salary, but he turned me down. He's got his pride," he said.

Ernesto nodded. "I hear you, homie. It's gotta be hard."

"You can't imagine, dude. How would you feel if your father wasn't a fine history teacher making a good salary and taking care of his family, if, instead, he was going around looking for cans so he could buy a little something to ease the misery of being him. Dad's got aches and pains. He's had a lot of injuries, but the deepest one is to his pride. He's told me a hundred times how sorry he is that I gotta use some of my salary to pay for our food and gas and electric. Every time he looks at my rusty old beater of a truck, he's got pain in his face like if it wasn't for him, I'd be driving decent wheels," Julio said.

"Julio, is there anything—" Ernesto started to ask.

Julio cut in. "No, there's nothing you can do, dude. I know you'd help in any way you could, but how do you think Pop would feel if I started begging money from my friends? I think he'd jump in the river. But look, Ernie, you're a great friend, and if it wasn't for your friendship, maybe *I'd* jump in the river."

"Well, maybe something will come up, like some little job he could do that wouldn't be too hard and would put a few extra bucks in his pocket," Ernesto said.

"Yeah," Julio said. "Maybe the tooth fairy will offer him a gig, or maybe a genie will leap from one of those dirty soda bottles and ask him to make a wish." There was bitterness in Julio's voice.

"Sorry, man," Ernesto said. It was all he could think of to say.

As Julio headed for his first class, he met Rod Garcia coming from the oppo-site direction. Ever since the Griff Slocum incident, Rod had been subdued. Ordinarily he would have made some snide remark, but he said nothing.

Julio didn't think Rod's manners would last long, but the juvenile court was currently trying to decide if they should level charges against the three boys for concealing information about the incident.

Rod wasn't eager to make any waves or any more enemies just now.

Abel Ruiz came along and fell in step with Julio. "How's it going, man?" Abel asked. "You look like your dog just died."

"My pop was rooting around in the dumpsters this morning when I started my morning run. The poor guy likes a little spending money, and our budget is pretty tight. It's like a knife turning in me to see him like that, you know?" Julio said. Abel briefly threw an arm around Julio's shoulders. He didn't say a word. Julio continued, "The hardest part is what it's doing to my father. He's so ashamed of where he's at. I tell him he's a good pop and that I wouldn't exchange him for anybody, but he's so *broken.*"

"Yeah, homie, I get what you're saying. At my house, it's not that bad, but I get to see my father feeling like a piece of dirt too, man. When he and Mom got married, he lost his job and had to beg Mom's cousin for work. Mom kept reminding him of how wonderful and generous her relatives are, and how lucky he is that they let him break his back every day. Dad did hard, dirty work, and he had a better sense of how to landscape a yard. He's had ideas better than the dudes he worked for, but Mom wouldn't let him make any suggestions. She was afraid her wonderful relatives would resent that."

Abel was on a roll. "Julio, I saw my father shrinking every day, little by little, going down like a burning candle. So I know where you're coming from. Since that drunkard hit him, though, he's been on disability, and I'm telling you, it's the best thing that's happened to him in twenty years. I'm hoping the lawyers get him a good settlement. Me and him actually go fishing now, for the first time in my life!"

Julio smiled and high-fived Abel. "Good luck to your dad and you, homie."

As Julio walked on, he knew that Abel understood the pain in the Avila family more than Ernesto Sandoval ever could. Ernie had a big heart, but unless you've experienced it, you don't understand how a good man can be whittled down to nothing.

Bianca Marquez was back in school and looking better than anybody could remember her ever looking. She was still too thin, but her arms didn't look like sticks anymore. And when she came with Abel to lunch at noon, she smiled at the gang and didn't just want to eat lettuce leaves like she did before. She actually ate a sandwich Abel had made for her: Swiss cheese, sliced corned beef, and creamy deli coleslaw on the side.

"This is sooo good," Bianca exulted.

Ernesto, Naomi, Carmen, and Mona,

Julio's girlfriend, also came, but there was no sign of Julio.

"No Julio?" Ernesto asked Mona Lisa.

"Poor Julio, he was feeling bad," Mona said. "He's worried about his dad. Poor Mr. Avila is really down on his luck, and that hurts Julio."

"Life can be a bear," Abel said. "So many creeps are living large, and a poor dude like Mr. Avila … he showed so much compassion for Griff Slocum, and still he gets the dirty end of the stick."

"I heard Rick Alanzar and Humberto Gomez are going to have to do community service for not telling the law everything they knew. Rod Garcia isn't involved because he wasn't there the night Rob Gomez kinda showed his hand. Gomez swears he never dreamed his uncle was the killer, but Rick sorta always had suspicions. The thing is, those three guys have got to live with something for the rest of their lives. If they hadn't hassled Mr. Slocum, the murder would not have happened," Ernesto said.

"I hope they have to clean toilets in the park for the rest of the year," Naomi said. "I think that would be good community service for them. Have any of you guys been to the park restrooms in a while?"

Abel laughed. "That's good, and then let them clean up the dog park every afternoon."

"I'm trying to eat my delicious sandwich," Bianca groaned.

"I wonder how Mrs. Slocum is doing," Ernesto said. "I looked up the value of a Honus Wagner in the collectibles book, and even if it's kinda ragged, it's probably worth a couple hundred thousand."

"I think the lady is already wealthy," Abel said. "She lives in a gated community up in LA. The rich get richer and the poor … well, you know the rest."

"Julio told me she tried to help her son," Mona said. "She went to visit Mr. Avila and Julio when her son was killed—before they knew who did it. She said her son would hide from her, not let her know where he was. He was so ashamed of his life, he didn't want to see her. He said he'd call her once in a while but that was all."

"Rich ladies kinda make me sick," Abel said.

"You're in kind of a bad mood, aren't you, Abel?" Naomi said.

"Yeah, I guess," Abel said. "Mom is fawning over Tomás again. He'll be coming down soon to brag about his newest academic honor. It's like when he comes in the house, there's a drumroll in the air. I see him coming, and I want to puke. I wish he'd move to the Fiji Islands and become king of some primitive tribe and leave us alone."

Naomi thought about her own three rough-and-tumble brothers. She was grateful for their down-to-earth qualities. Orlando, the oldest, was all over the Internet with his new music, and he and Manny were riding high. But they were never arrogant. Ernesto felt grateful too that there wasn't some incredible older brother in his family, excelling so much at everything that he couldn't possibly measure up.

"Your mom doesn't mean to play favorites, Abel," Naomi pointed out. "I'm sure she loves you and Penelope as much as Tomás."

"Naomi," Abel said, "you don't get it. I'm just waiting for the day she rolls out a red carpet for him to walk into the house on."

Bianca laughed. It dawned on everybody that they'd never seen her laugh so heartily before. Maybe it was because she was hungry all the time. Then Bianca said, "Abel, in my house, I'm pretty much of a nobody too. Mom only has eyes for her new husband. I don't know what she sees in him, but he's the center of her universe. He's homely, but he makes good money. I guess that's part of it. I'm just counting the days when I graduate from here and can go off to college and never have to live with them again."

Abel looked at the girl sympathetically.

"I'm looking forward to going to culinary school in another town. I got a scholarship already. I'll be living there and getting started on my real life. Then Mom can worship Tomás all she likes. My only regret is that I'll be leaving Penelope to fend for herself, but she's tough and strong. It's not as bad for her to have Mom drooling over Tomás. Penelope is a girl, and she doesn't feel the sibling rivalry I feel. And then I guess I'll be coming home to visit quite a bit. I wanna check on my dad and Penny too. She's a big pest most of the time, but I love the little gnome."

Ernesto looked at his friend and smiled. "And you can't forget your homies, Abel. I'll be going to City College and then State, and I'll be living at home to save money. I don't want some huge student loan on my back when I graduate. So you gotta drop by Wren Street every once in a while, or I'll go up to that culinary school and haunt you, man."

"I'll never cut you off, homie," Abel

said. "You're for the long run. When we're broken-down old men, we'll be hanging out together cursing our fates."

"I'm going to City College too," Naomi said. "It's so much cheaper to do the first two years there, then State."

Ernesto reached over and covered Naomi's hand with his. "We'll be together, babe."

"Yeah," Abel said, "you got that perfect family over there on Wren Street, Ernie. It's easy living with them. And, Naomi … uh, you got a nice mom and … and a really nice pit bull there."

When Julio got home from school that day, his father seemed to be in a state of shock. He was sitting in the little trailer, at the dinette table, with an opened letter on his lap.

"What's the matter, Pop?" Julio asked. "Bad news?" Julio couldn't imagine a letter that some relative had died. They didn't have any relatives. In spite of their poverty, they didn't owe any big bills so nobody should be harassing them.

"Julio," his father stammered. "It's from a lawyer—"

"A lawyer?" Julio repeated. "Somebody suing us, Pop? They must be crazy. You can't squeeze blood out of a turnip, and that's what we got here. Turnips."

"I don't understand it, Julio. Would you read the letter and see what's going on? I don't understand it," Mr. Avila said. His hands were shaking.

Julio took the letter along with some documents. He read the letter and his legs got so weak he had to sit down at the dinette table across from his father. "Pop," he said, "it's from Mrs. Slocum's lawyer. You know, Griff Slocum's mother. She arranged it so you get an annuity every month from next month on."

"A *what?*" Mr. Avila asked.

"An annuity. You get a thousand dollars every month for as long as you live. And she paid for a life insurance policy so when you're a hundred and five and you check out for heaven, I get a big sum of money," Julio said.

He started to laugh and cry at the same time. He grabbed his father's shoulders and said, "Pop, a thousand bucks every month! You can buy a hundred chocolate bars."

Tears filled Mr. Avila's eyes, "But I don't understand. Why would she do such a thing?"

"She says in the letter that this annuity comes from the Honus Wagner baseball card. You remember when she came to see us? She said you were the only friend her son had. You were the only one who took him out for fish and chips and beer once in a while and treated him like a human being. She did this to thank you for being kind to her son, Pop. You get a thousand a month, and you won't have to look for cans and bottles in dumpsters anymore … not *ever*."

"But, what must I do to earn it?" Mr. Avila said.

"Nothing, Pop. Just enjoy. You earned it when you saved up money for weeks so you'd have enough to give Griff Slocum a little treat. She says here in the letter that the Honus Wagner belonged to her son, and that he would want his friend to have some of the benefit from his treasure."

Julio hugged his father, and they sat there for several hours, crying a little, laughing a lot, reading and rereading the letter.

On Washington Street, Mr. Hussam also received a letter from Mrs. Slocum's lawyer. There was a generous check made out to Mr. Hussam. It was more money than Mr. Hussam had ever received for anything. Shaking with emotion, he read the woman's words: "My son had no place to lay his head, but you sheltered him behind your store. You allowed him to use the restroom facilities in your store. You showed him kindness, and I thank you with all my heart. Accept this gift with my gratitude. Consider it from my son—his final gift."

They later learned that the proceeds from the sale of the Honus Wagner baseball card had gone to Mr. Avila's annuity and the gift to Mr. Hussam; with the considerable amount that was left over, Mrs. Slocum endowed a local scholarship fund. It was the largest bequest the fund had ever received, and it meant scholarships for numerous young people in the *barrio* for years to come.

On a bright, sunlit day a few weeks later, the Sandovals, Martinezes, Ruizes, and all of their extended family and friends gathered to hear Councilman Emilio Zapata Ibarra unveil a new commemorative plaque at Chavez High.

In honor of Griff Slocum,
for the education of the
young people who graduate
from Cesar Chavez High School.
— Laura Slocum

"Turns out Griff accomplished something after all," Mr. Ibarra said. "A bright future for so many kids. His Honus Wagner was a treasure beyond what he knew."

"I wish Griff were here to see this," somebody said.

Ernesto hugged Naomi against him and smiled at her. "He knows," Ernesto said. "He knows."